If I May

A. A. Milne

If I May

The present edition is a reproduction of previous publication of this classic work. Minor typographical errors may have been corrected without note; however, for an authentic reading experience the spelling, punctuation, and capitalization have been retained from the original text.

ISBN: 978-1-63637-477-2

CONTENTS

THE CASE FOR THE ARTIST 1
A LONDON GARDEN 5
THE GAME OF KINGS 8
FIXTURES AND FITTINGS 12
EXPERTS 15
THE ROBINSON TRADITION 18
GETTING THINGS DONE 22
CHRISTMAS GAMES 25
THE MATHEMATICAL MIND 28
GOING OUT TO DINNER 31
THE ETIQUETTE OF ESCAPE 36
GEOGRAPHICAL RESEARCH 39
CHILDREN'S PLAYS 42
THE ROAD TO KNOWLEDGE 46
A MAN OF PROPERTY 49
AN ORDNANCE MAP 52
THE LORD MAYOR 55
THE HOLIDAY PROBLEM 59
THE BURLINGTON ARCADE 62
STATE LOTTERIES 65
THE RECORD LIE 68
WEDDING BELLS 71
PUBLIC OPINION 76
THE HONOUR OF YOUR COUNTRY 79
A VILLAGE CELEBRATION 85
A TRAIN OF THOUGHT 89
MELODRAMA 92
A LOST MASTERPIECE 95
A HINT FOR NEXT CHRISTMAS 98
THE FUTURE 103
THE LARGEST CIRCULATION 106

THE WATSON TOUCH 109

SOME OLD COMPANIONS 112

A HAUNTED HOUSE 115

ROUND THE WORLD AND BACK 118

THE STATE OF THE THEATRE 121

THE FIRES OF AUTUMN 125

NOT GUILTY 128

A DIGRESSION 131

HIGH FINANCE 134

SECRET PAPERS 138

The Case for the Artist

By an "artist" I mean Shakespeare and Me and Bach and Myself and Velasquez and Phidias, and even You if you have ever written four lines on the sunset in somebody's album, or modelled a Noah's Ark for your little boy in plasticine. Perhaps we have not quite reached the heights where Shakespeare stands, but we are on his track. Shakespeare can be representative of all of us, or Velasquez if you prefer him. One of them shall be President of our United Artists' Federation. Let us, then, consider what place in the scheme of things our federation can claim.

Probably we artists have all been a little modest about ourselves lately. During the war we asked ourselves gloomily what use we were to the State compared with the noble digger of coals, the much-to-be-reverenced maker of boots, and the god-like grower of wheat. Looking at the pictures in the illustrated papers of brawny, half-dressed men pushing about blocks of red-hot iron, we have told ourselves that these heroes were the pillars of society, and that we were just an incidental decoration. It was a wonder that we were allowed to live. And now in these days of strikes, when a single union of manual workers can hold up the rest of the nation, it is a bitter reflection to us that, if we were to strike, the country would go on its way quite happily, and nine-tenths of the population would not even know that we had downed our pens and brushes.

If there is any artist who has been depressed by such thoughts as these, let him take comfort. We are all right.

I made the discovery that we were all right by studying the life of the bee. All that I knew about bees until yesterday was derived from that great naturalist, Dr. Isaac Watts. In common with every one who has been a child I knew that the insect in question improved each shining hour by something honey something something every something flower. I had also heard that bees could not sting you if you held your breath, a precaution which would make conversation by the herbaceous border an affair altogether too spasmodic; and, finally, that in any case the same bee could only sting you once—though, apparently, there was no similar provision of Nature's that the same person could not be stung twice.

Well, that was all that I knew about bees until yesterday. I used to see them about the place from time to time, busy enough, no doubt, but really no busier than I was; and as they were not much interested in me they had no reason to complain that I was not much interested in them. But since yesterday, when I read a book which dealt fully, not only with the public life of the bee, but with the most intimate details of its private life, I have looked at them with a new interest and a new sympathy. For there is no animal which does not get more out of life than the pitiable insect which Dr. Watts holds up as an example to us.

Hitherto, it may be, you have thought of the bee as an admirable and industrious insect, member of a model community which worked day and night to but one end—the well-being of the coming race. You knew perhaps that it fertilized the flowers, but you also knew that the bee didn't know; you were aware that, it any bee deliberately went about trying to improve your delphiniums instead of gathering honey for the State, it would be turned down promptly by the other workers. For nothing is done in the hive without this one utilitarian purpose. Even the drones take their place in the scheme of things; a minor place in the stud; and when the next generation is assured, and the drones cease to be useful and can now only revert to the ornamental, they are ruthlessly cast out.

It comes, then, to this. The bee devotes its whole life to preparing for the next generation. But what is the next generation going to do? It is going to spend its whole life preparing for the third generation... and so on for ever.

An admirable community, the moralists tell us. Poor moralists! To

2

miss so much of the joy of life; to deny oneself the pleasure (to mention only one among many) of reclining lazily on one's back in a snap-dragon, watching the little white clouds sail past upon a sea of blue; to miss these things for no other reason than that the next generation may also have an opportunity of missing them—is that admirable? What do the bees think that they are doing? If they live a life of toil and self-sacrifice merely in order that the next generation may live a life of equal toil and self-sacrifice, what has been gained? Ask the next bee you meet what it thinks it is doing in this world, and the only answer it can give you is, "Keeping up the supply of bees." Is that an admirable answer? How much more admirable if it could reply that it was eschewing all pleasure and living the life of a galley-slave in order that the next generation might have leisure to paint the poppy a more glorious scarlet. But no. The next generation is going at it just as hard for the same unproductive end; it has no wish to leave anything behind it—a new colour, a new scent, a new idea. It has one object only in this world—more bees. Could any scheme of life be more sterile?

Having come to this conclusion about the bee, I took fresh courage. I saw at once that it was the artist in Man which made him less contemptible than the Bee. That god-like person the grower of wheat assumed his proper level. Bread may be necessary to existence, but what is the use of existence if you are merely going to employ it in making bread? True, the farmer makes bread, not only for himself, but for the miner; and the miner produces coal—not only for himself, but for the farmer; and the farmer also produces bread for the maker of boots, who produces boots, not only for himself, but for the farmer and the miner. But you are still getting no further. It is the Life of the Bee over again, with no other object in it but mere existence. If this were all, there would be nothing to write on our tombstones but "Born 1800; Died 1880. He lived till then."

But it is not all, because—and here I strike my breast proudly—because of us artists. Not only can we write on Shakespeare's tomb, "He wrote Hamlet" or "He was not for an age, but for all time," but we can write on a contemporary baker's tomb, "He provided bread for the man who wrote Hamlet," and on a contemporary butcher's tomb, "He was not only for himself, but for Shakespeare." We perceive, in fact, that the only matter upon which any worker, other than the artist, can congratulate himself, whether he be manual-worker, brain-worker, surgeon, judge, or politician, is that he is helping to make the world tolerable for the artist. It is only the artist who will leave anything behind him. He is the fighting-man, the man who counts; the others are merely the Army Service Corps of civilization. A world without its artists, a world of bees, would be as futile and as meaningless a thing as an army composed entirely of the A.S.C.

Possibly you put in a plea here for the explorer and the scientist. The explorer perhaps may stand alone. His discovery of a peak in Darien is something in itself, quite apart from the happy possibility that Keats may be tempted to bring it into a sonnet. Yes, if a Beef-Essence-Merchant has only provided sustenance for an Explorer he has not lived in vain, however much the poets and the painters recoil from his wares. But of the scientist I am less certain. I fancy that his invention of the telephone (for instance) can only be counted to his credit because it has brought the author into closer touch with his publisher.

So we artists (yes, and explorers) may be of good faith. They may try to pretend, these others, in their little times of stress, that we are nothing—decorative, inessential; that it is they who make the world go round. This will not upset us. We could not live without them; true. But (a much more bitter thought) they would have no reason for living at all, were it not for us.

A London Garden

I have always wanted a garden of my own. Other people's gardens are all very well, but the visitor never sees them at their best. He comes down in June, perhaps, and says something polite about the roses. "You ought to have seen them last year," says his host disparagingly, and the visitor represses with difficulty the retort, "You ought to have asked me down to see them last year." Or, perhaps, he comes down in August, and lingers for a moment beneath the fig-tree. "Poor show of figs," says the host, "I don't know what's happened to them. Now we had a record crop of raspberries. Never seen them so plentiful before." And the visitor has to console himself with the thought of the raspberries which he has never seen, and will probably miss again next year. It is not very comforting.

Give me, therefore, a garden of my own. Let me grow my own flowers, and watch over them from seedhood to senility. Then shall I miss nothing of their glory, and when visitors come I can impress them with my stories of the wonderful show of groundsel which we had last year.

For the moment I am contenting myself with groundsel. To judge by the present state of the garden, the last owner must have prided himself chiefly on his splendid show of canaries. Indeed, it would not surprise me to hear that he referred to his garden as "the back-yard." This would take the heart out of anything which was trying to flower there, and it is only natural that, with the exception of the three groundsel beds, the garden is now a wilderness. Perhaps "wilderness" gives you a misleading impression of space, the actual size of the pleasaunce being about two hollyhocks by one, but it is the correct word to describe the air of neglect which hangs over the place. However, I am going to alter that.

With a garden of this size, though, one has to be careful. One cannot decide lightly upon a croquet-lawn here, an orchard there, and a rockery in the corner; one has to go all out for the one particular thing, whether it is the last hoop and the stick of a croquet-lawn, a mulberry-tree, or an herbaceous border. Which do we want most— a fruit garden, a flower garden, or a water garden? Sometimes I think fondly of a water garden, with a few perennial gold-fish flashing swiftly across it, and ourselves walking idly by the margin and pointing them out to our visitors; and then I realize sadly that, by the time an adequate margin has been provided for ourselves and our visitors, there will be no room left for the gold-fish.

At the back of my garden I have a high brick wall. To whom the bricks actually belong I cannot say, but at any rate I own the surface rights on this side of it. One of my ideas is to treat it as the back cloth of a stage, and paint a vista on it. A long avenue of immemorial elms, leading up to a gardener's lodge at the top of the wall—I mean at the end of the avenue—might create a pleasing impression. My workroom leads out into the garden, and I have a feeling that, if the door of this room were opened, and then hastily closed again on the plea that I mustn't be disturbed, a visitor might obtain such a glimpse of the avenue and the gardener's lodge as would convince him that I had come into property. He might even make an offer for the estate, if he were set upon a country house in the heart of London.

But you have probably guessed already the difficulty in the way of my vista. The back wall extends into the gardens of the householders on each side of me. They might refuse to co-operate with me; they might insist on retaining the blank ugliness of theirs walls, or endeavouring (as they endeavour now, I believe) to grow some unenterprising creeper up them; with the result that my vista would fail to create the necessary illusion when looked at from the side. This would mean that our guests would have to remain in one position, and that even in this position they would have to stand to attention—a state of things which might mar their enjoyment of our hospitality. Until, then, our neighbours give me a free hand with their segments of the wall, the vista must remain a beautiful dream.

However, there are other possibilities. Since there is no room in the garden for a watchdog and a garden, it might be a good idea to paint a phosphorescent and terrifying watchdog on the wall. Perhaps a watchlion would be even more terrifying—and, presumably, just as easy to paint. Any burglar would be deterred if he came across a lion suddenly in the back garden. One way or another, it should be possible to have something a little more interesting than mere bricks at the end of the estate.

And if the worst comes to the worst—if it is found that no flowers (other than groundsel) will flourish in my garden, owing to lack of soil or lack of sun—then the flowers must be painted on the walls. This would have its advantages, for we should waste no time over the early and uninteresting stages of the plant, but depict it at once in its full glory. And we should keep our garden up to date. When delphiniums went out of season, we should rub them out and give you chrysanthemums; and if an untimely storm uprooted the chrysanthemums, in an hour or two we should have a wonderful show of dahlias to take their place. And we should still have the floor-space free for a sundial, or—if you insist on exercise—for the last hoop and the stick of a full-sized croquet-lawn.

The Game of Kings

I do not claim to be an authority on either the history or the practice of chess, but, as the poet Gray observed when he saw his old school from a long way off, it is sometimes an advantage not to know too much of one's subject. The imagination can then be exercised more effectively. So when I am playing Capablanca (or old Robinson) for the championship of the home pastures, my thoughts are not fixed exclusively upon the "mate" which is threatening; they wander off into those enchanted lands of long ago, when flesh-and-blood knights rode at stone-built castles, and thin-lipped bishops, all smiles and side-long glances, plotted against the kings who ventured to oppose them. This is the real fascination of chess.

You observe that I speak of castles, not of rooks. I do not know whence came this custom of calling the most romantic piece on the board by the name of a very ordinary bird, but I, at least, will not be a party to it. I refuse to surrender the portcullis and the moat, the bastion and the well-manned towers, which were the features of every castle with which hitherto I have played, in order to take the field with allies so unromantic as a brace of rooks. You may tell me that "rook" is a corruption of this or that word, meaning something which has never laid an egg in its life. It may be so, but in that case you cannot blame me for continuing to call it the castle which its shape proclaims it.

Knowing nothing of the origin of the game, I can tell myself stories about it. That it was invented by a woman is obvious, for why else should the queen be the most powerful piece of them all? She lived, this woman, in a priest-ridden land, but she had no love for the Church. Neither bland white bishop nor crooked-smiling black bishop did she love; that is why she made them move sideways. Yet she could not deny them their power. They were as powerful as the gallant young knight who rode past her window singing to battle, where he swooped upon the enemy impetuously from this side and that, heedless of the obstacles in the way, or worked two of them into such a position that, though one might escape, the other was doomed to bite the dust. Yet the bishop, man of peace though he proclaimed himself, was as powerful as he, but not so powerful as a baron in his well-fortified castle. For sometimes there were places beyond the influence of the Church, if one could reach them in safety; though when the Church hunted in couples, the king's priest and the queen's priest out together, then there was no certain refuge, and one must sally upon them bravely and run the risk of being excommunicated.

No, she did not love the Church. Sometimes I think that she was herself a queen, who had suffered at the hands of the bishops; and, just as you or I put our enemies into a book, thereby gaining much private satisfaction even though they do not recognize themselves, so she made a game of her enemies and enjoyed her revenge in secret. But if she were a queen, then she was a queen-mother, and the king was not her husband but her little son. This would account for the perpetual intrigues against him, and the fact that he was so powerless to aid himself. Probably the enemy was too strong for him in the end, and he and his mother were taken into captivity together. It was in prison that she invented the royal game, the young king amused himself by carving out the first rough pieces.

But was she a queen? Sometimes I think that I have the story wrong; for what queen in those days would have assented to a proposition so democratic as that a man-at-arms (a "pawn" in the language of the unromantic) could rise by his own exertions to the dignity of Royalty itself? But if she were a waiting-maid in love with the king's own man-at-arms, then it would be natural that she should set no limit to her ambitions for him. The man-at-arms crowned would be in keeping with her most secret dreams.

These are the things of which I think when I push my king's man-at-arms two leagues forward. A game of chess is a romance sport when it is described in that dull official notation "P to K4 Kt to KB3"; a story should be woven around it. One of these days,

9

perhaps, I shall tell the story of my latest defeat. Lewis Carroll had some such intention when he began Alice Through the Looking Glass, but he went at it half-heartedly. Besides, being a clergyman and writing as he did for children, he was handicapped; he dared not introduce the bishops. I shall have no such fears, and my story will be serious.

Consider for a moment the romance which underlies the most ordinary game. You push out the king's pawn and your opponent does the same. It is plain (is it not?) that these are the heralds, meeting at the border-line between the two kingdoms—Ivoria and Ebonia, let us say. There I have my first chapter: The history of the dispute, the challenge by Ivoria, the acceptance of the challenge by Ebonia. Chapter Two describes the sallying forth of the knights— "Kt to KB3, Kt to QB3." In the next chapter the bishop gains the queen's ear and suggests that he should take the field. He is no fighter, but he has the knack of excommunicating. The queen, a young and beautiful widow, with an infant son, consents ("B to QB4"), and set about removing her child to a place of safety. She invokes the aid of Roqueblanc, an independent chieftain, who, spurred on by love for her, throws all his forces on to her side, offering at the same time his well-guarded fastness as a sanctuary for her boy. ("Castles.") Then the queen musters all her own troops and leads them into battle by the side of the Baron Roqueblanc....

But I must not tell you the whole story now. You can imagine for yourself some of the more exciting things which happen. You can picture, for instance, that vivid chapter in which the young king, at a moment when his very life is threatened by an Ebonian baron, is saved by the self-sacrifices of Roqueblanc, who hurls himself in front of the royal youth's person and himself falls a victim, to be avenged immediately by a watchful man-at-arms. You can follow, if you will, the further adventures of that man-at-arms, up to that last chapter when he marries the still beautiful queen, and henceforward acts in her name, taking upon himself a power similar to her own. In fact, you can write the book yourself. But if you do not care to do this, let me beg you at least to bring a little

10

imagination to the next game which you play. Then whether you win or (as is more likely) you lose, you will at least be worthy of the Game of Kings.

Fixtures and Fittings

There was once a young man who decided to be a poodle-clipper. He felt that he had a natural bent for it, and he had been told that a fashionable poodle-clipper could charge his own price for his services. But his father urged him to seek another profession. "It is an uncertain life, poodle-clipping," he said, "To begin with, very few people keep poodles at all. Of these few, only a small proportion wants its poodles clipped. And, of this small proportion, a still smaller proportion is likely to want its poodles clipped by you." So the young man decided to be a hair-dresser instead.

I thought of this story the other day when I was bargaining with a house-agent about "fixtures," and I decided that no son of mine should become a curtain-pole manufacturer. I suppose that the price of a curtain-rod (pole or perch) is only a few shillings, and, once made, it remains in a house for ever. Tenants come and go, new landlords buy and sell, but the old brass rod stays firm at the top of the window, supporting curtain after curtain. How many new sets are made in a year? No more, it would seem, than the number of new houses built. Far better, then to manufacture an individual possession like a tooth-brush, which has the additional advantage of wearing out every few months.

But from the consumer's point of view, a curtain-rod is a pleasant thing. He has the satisfaction of feeling that, having once bought it, he has bought it for the rest of his life. He may change his house and with it his Fixtures, but there is no loss on the brass part of the transaction, however much there may be on the bricks and mortar. What he pays out with one hand, he takes in with the other. Nor is his property subject to the ordinary mischances of life. There was an historic character who "lost the big drum," but he would become even more historic who had lost a curtain-rod, and neither parlour-maid nor cat is ever likely to wear a guilty conscience over the breaking of one.

I have not yet discovered, in spite of my recent familiarity with house-agents, the difference between a fixture and a fitting. It is possible that neither word has any virtue without the other, as is the case with "spick" and "span." One has to be both; however dapper, one would never be described as a span gentleman. In the same way it may be that a curtain-rod or an electric light is never just a fixture or a fitting, but always "included in the fixtures and fittings." Then there is a distinction, apparently, between a "landlord's fixture" and a "tenant's fixture," which is rather subtle. A fire-dog is a landlord's fixture; so is a door-plate. If you buy a house you get the fire-dogs and the door-plates thrown in, which seems unnecessarily generous. I can understand the landlord deciding to throw in the walls and the roof, because he couldn't do much with them if you refused to take them, but it is a mystery why he should include a door-plate, which can easily be removed and sold to somebody else. And if a door-plate, why not a curtain-rod? A curtain-rod is a necessity to the incoming tenant; a door-plate is merely a luxury for the grubby- fingered to help them to keep the paint clean. One might be expected to bring one's own door-plate with one, according to the size of one's hand.

For the whole idea of a fixture or fitting can only be that it is something about which there can be no individual taste. We furnish a house according to our own private fancy; the "fixtures" are the furnishings in regard to which we are prepared to accept the general fancy. The other man's curtain-rod, though easily detachable and able to fit a hundred other windows, is a fixture; his carpet-as-planned (to use the delightful language of the house-agent), though securely nailed down and the wrong size for any other room but this, is not a fixture. Upon some such reasoning the first authorized schedule of fixtures and fittings must have been made out.

It seems a pity that it has not been extended. There are other things than curtain-rods and electric-light bulbs which might be left behind in the old house and picked up again in the new. The silver cigarette-box, which we have all had as a birthday or wedding

13

present, might safely be handed over to the incoming tenant, in the certainty that another just like it will be waiting for us in our next house. True, it will have different initials on it, but that will only make it the more interesting, our own having become fatiguing to us by this time. Possibly this sort of thing has already been done in an unofficial way among neighbors. By mutual agreement they leave their aspidistras and their "Maiden's Prayer" behind them. It saves trouble and expense in the moving, which is an important thing in these days, and there would always be the hope that the next aspidistra might be on the eve of flowering or laying eggs, or whatever it is that its owner expects from it.

Experts

The man in front of the fire was telling us a story about his wife and a bottle of claret. He had taken her to the best restaurant in Paris and had introduced her to a bottle of the famous Chateau Whatsitsname, 1320 (or thereabouts), a wine absolutely priceless— although the management, with its customary courtesy, had allowed him to pay a certain amount for it. Not realizing that it was actually the famous Whatsitsname, she had drunk it in the ordinary way, neither holding it up to the light and saying, "Ah, there's a wine!" nor rolling it round the palate before swallowing. On the next day they went to a commonplace restaurant and drank a local and contemporary vintage at five francs the bottle, of similar colour but very different temperament. When she had finished her glass, she said hesitatingly, "Of course, I don't know anything about wine, and I dare say I'm quite wrong, but I can't help feeling that the claret we had last night was better than this."

The man in front of the fire was rather amused by this, as were most of his audience. For myself, I felt that the lady demanded my admiration rather than my amusement. Without the assistance of the labels, many of us might have decided that it was the five-franc vintage which was the better wine. She didn't. Indeed, I am inclined to read more into the story than is perhaps there; I believe that she had misunderstood her husband, and had thought that the second bottle was the famous, aged, and priceless Chateau Whatsitsname, and that, in spite of this, she gave it as her opinion that the first wine, cheap and modern though it might be, was the better. Hats off, then, to a brave woman! How many of us would have her courage and her honesty?

But perhaps you who read this are an expert on wine. If so, you are lucky. I am an expert on nothing—nothing, anyhow, that matters. I envy all you experts tremendously. When I see a cigar-expert listening to his cigar before putting it in his mouth I wish that I were as great a man as he. Privately sometimes I have listened to a cigar, but it has told me nothing. The only way I can tell whether it is good or bad is by smoking it. Even then I could not tell you (without the assistance of the band) whether it was a Sancho Panza or a Guoco Piano. I could only tell you whether I liked it or not, a question of no importance whatever.

Lately I have been trying to become a furniture-expert, but it is a disheartening business. I have a book called Chats on Old Furniture—a terrible title to have to ask for in a shop, but I asked boldly. Perhaps the word "chat" does not make other people feel as unhappy as it makes me. But even after reading this book I am not really an expert. I know now that it is no good listening to a Chippendale chair to see if it is really Chippendale; one must stroke it in order to find out whether it is a "genuine antique" or only a modern reproduction; but it is obvious that years of stroking would be necessary before an article of furniture would be properly responsive. Is it worth while wasting these years of one's life? Indeed, is it worth while (I ask nervously) bothering whether a chair or a table is antique or modern so long as it is both useful and beautiful?

Well, let me tell you what happened to us yesterday. We found a dresser which appealed to us considerably, and we stood in front of it, looking at it. We decided that except for a little curley-wiggle at the top it was the jolliest dresser we had seen, "That's a fine old dresser," said the shopman, coming up at that moment, and he smacked it encouragingly. "A really fine old dresser, that." We agreed. "Except for those curley-wiggles," I added, pointing to them with my umbrella. "If we could take those off." He looked at me reproachfully. "You wouldn't take those off——" he said. "Why, that's what tells you that it's a Welsh dresser of 1720." We didn't buy that dresser. We decided that the size or the price was all wrong. But I wonder now, supposing we had bought it, whether we should have had the pluck to remove the curley-wiggles (and let people mistake it for an English dresser of 1920) in order that, so abbreviated, it might have been more beautiful.

16

For furniture is not beautiful merely because it is old. It is absurd to suppose that everything made in 1720—or 1620 or 1520—was made beautifully, as it would be absurd to say that everything made in 1920 was beautiful. No doubt there will always be people who will regard the passing of time as sufficient justification for any article of furniture; I could wish that they were equally tolerant among the arts as among the crafts, so that in 2120 this very article which I write now could be referred to with awe as a genuine 1920; but all that the passage of time can really do for your dresser is to give a more beautiful surface and tone to the wood. This, surely, is a matter which you can judge for yourself without being an expert. If your dresser looks old you have got from it all that age can give you; if it looks beautiful you have got from it all that a craftsman of any period can give you; why worry, then, as to whether or not it is a "genuine antique"? The expert may tell you that it is a fake, but the fact that he has suddenly said so has not made your dining-room less beautiful. Or if it is less beautiful, it is only because an "expert" is now in it. Hurry him out.

The Robinson Tradition

Having read lately an appreciation of that almost forgotten author Marryat, and having seen in the shilling box of a second-hand bookseller a few days afterward a copy of Masterman Ready, I went in and bought the same. I had read it as a child, and remembered vaguely that it combined desert-island adventure with a high moral tone; jam and powder in the usual proportions. Reading it again, I found that the powder was even more thickly spread than I had expected; hardly a page but carried with it a valuable lesson for the young; yet this particular jam (guava and cocoanut) has such an irresistible attraction for me that I swallowed it all without a struggle, and was left with a renewed craving for more and yet more desert-island stories. Having, unfortunately, no others at hand, the only satisfaction I can give myself is to write about them.

I would say first that, even if an author is writing for children (as was Marryat), and even if morality can best be implanted in the young mind with a watering of fiction, yet a desert-island story is the last story which should be used for this purpose. For a desert-island is a child's escape from real life and its many lessons. Ask yourself why you longed for a desert-island when you were young, and you will find the answer to be that you did what you liked there, ate what you liked, and carried through your own adventures. It is the "Family" which spoils The Swiss Family Robinson, just as it is the Seagrave family which nearly wrecks Masterman Ready. What is the good of imagining yourself (as every boy does) "Alone in the Pacific" if you are not going to be alone? Well, perhaps we do not wish to be quite alone; but certainly to have more than two on an island is to overcrowd it, and our companion must be of a like age and disposition.

For this reason parents spoil any island for a healthy-minded boy. He may love his father and mother as fondly as even they could wish, but he does not want to take them bathing in the lagoon with him—still less to have them on the shore, telling him that there are too many sharks this morning and that it is quite time he came out. Nor for that matter do parents want to be bothered with children on a South Sea holiday. In Masterman Ready there is a horrid little boy called Tommy, aged six, who is always letting the musket off accidentally, or getting bitten by a turtle, or taking more than his share of the cocoanut milk. As a grown-up I wondered why his father did not give him to the first savage who came by, and so allow himself a chance of enjoying his island in peace; but at Tommy's age I should have resented just as strongly a father who, even on a desert-island, could not bear to see his boy making a fool of himself with turtle and gunpowder.

I am not saying that a boy would really be happy for long, whether on a desert-island or elsewhere, without his father and mother. Indeed it is doubtful if he could survive, happily or unhappily. Possibly William Seagrave could have managed it. William was only twelve, but he talked like this: "I agree with you, Ready. Indeed I have been thinking the same thing for many days past.... I wish the savages would come on again, for the sooner they come the sooner the affair will be decided." A boy who can talk like this at twelve is capable of finding the bread-fruit tree for himself. But William is an exception. I claim no such independence for the ordinary boy; I only say that the ordinary boy, however dependent on his parents, does like to pretend that he is capable of doing without them, wherefore he gives them no leading part in the imaginary adventures which he pursues so ardently. If they are there at all, it is only that he may come back to them in the last chapter and tell them all about it... and be suitably admired.

Masterman Ready seems to me, then, to be the work of a father, not of an understanding writer for boys. Marryat wrote it for his own children, towards whom he had responsibilities; not for other people's children, for whom he would only be concerned to provide entertainment. But even if the book was meant for no wider circle than the home, one would still feel that the moral teaching was overdone. It should be possible to be edifying without losing one's sense of humour. When Juno, the black servant, was struck by lightning and not quite killed, she "appeared to be very sensible of the wonderful preservation which she had had. She had always been attentive whenever the Bible was read, but now she did not appear to think that the morning and evening services were sufficient to express her gratitude." Even a child would feel that Juno really need not have been struck by lightning at all; even a child might wonder how many services, on this scale of gratitude, were adequate for the rest of the party whom the lightning had completely missed. And it was perhaps a little self-centred of Ready to thank God for her recovery on the grounds that she could "ill be spared" by a family rather short-handed in the rainy season.

However, the story is the thing. As long as a desert-island book contains certain ingredients, I do not mind if other superfluous matter creeps in. Our demands—we of the elect who adore desert-islands—are simple. The castaways must build themselves a hut with the aid of a bag of nails saved from the wreck; they must catch turtles by turning them over on their backs; they must find the bread-fruit tree and have adventures with sharks. Twice they must be visited by savages. On the first occasion they are taken by surprise, but—the savages being equally surprised—no great harm is done. Then the Hero says, "They will return when the wind is favourable," and he arranges his defences, not forgetting to lay in a large stock of water. The savages return in force, and then—this is most important—at the most thirsty moment of the siege it is discovered that the water is all gone! Generally a stray arrow has pierced the water-butt, but in Masterman Ready the insufferable Tommy has played the fool with it. (He would.) This is the Hero's great opportunity. He ventures to the spring to get more water, and returns with it—wounded. Barely have the castaways wetted their lips with the precious fluid when the attack breaks out with redoubled fury. It seems now that all is lost... when, lo! a shell bursts into the middle of the attacking hordes. (Never into the middle of the defenders. That would be silly.) "Look," the Hero cries, "a vessel off-shore with its main braces set and a jib-sail flying" — or whatever it may be. And they return to London.

This is the story which we want, and we cannot have too many of them. Should you ever see any of us with our noses over the shilling box and an eager light in our eyes, you may be sure that we are on the track of another one.

Getting Things Done

In the castle of which I am honorary baron we are in the middle of an orgy of "getting things done." It must always be so, I suppose, when one moves into a new house. After the last furniture van has departed, and the painters' bill has been receipted, one feels that one can now settle down to enjoy one's new surroundings. But no. The discoveries begin. This door wants a new lock on it, that fireplace wants a brick taken out, the garden is in need of something else, somebody ought to inspect the cistern. What about the drains? There are a hundred things to be "done."

I have a method in these matters. When I observe that something wants doing, I say casually to the baroness, "We ought to do something about that fireplace," or whatever it is. I say it with the air of a man who knows exactly what to do, and would do it himself if he were not so infernally busy. The correct answer to this is, "Yes, I'll go and see about it to-day." Sometimes the baroness tries to put it on to me by saying, "We ought to do something about the cistern," but she has not quite got the casual tone necessary, and I have no difficulty in replying (with the air of a man who, etc.), "Yes, we ought." The proper answer to this is, "Very well, then. I'll go and see about it." In either case, as you will agree, action on the part of the baroness should follow.

Unfortunately it doesn't. She, it appears, is a partner in my weakness. We neither of us know how to get things done. It is a knowledge which one can never acquire. Either you are born with an instinct for the man round the corner who tests cisterns, or you are born without it, in which case you never, never find him. There are men with the instinct so highly developed that they can tell you at a moment's notice the name and address, not merely of a man who will test your cistern for you, but of the one man in your neighbourhood who will test it most efficiently and most cheaply. If your canary moulted unduly, and you said to your wife, "We must do something about Ambrose," they could tell you at once of the best canary-mender to approach. These are the men I admire. But there are weaklings (of both sexes, unfortunately) who would not even know whether a greengrocer or a veterinary surgeon was the man to send for, and who are entirely vague as to whether a cistern is tested for water or for lead-poisoning.

The press speaks of this or that politician sometimes as the "Minister who gets things done." I have always felt that, given an adequate permanent staff, I might go down to fame as the householder who got things done. As you see, my staff lets me down. I am quite capable of sitting in my office and saying to an under-secretary, "We must do something about this shell business." This, in fact, is just my line. I am quite capable of saying firmly, "I must have ten million big guns by August." And if the undersecretary only made the correct reply, "Very well, sir, I'll see about it," my photograph would appear in the papers as that of "the man who got the guns." But when your under-secretary refuses to carry on, where are you?

What I want, and what, I imagine, most people who have moved into a new house want, is an intermediary to get things done for us. I suggest this as a profession to any demobilized soldier looking for work. He should walk about London, making a note of the houses which have just been sold or let, and as soon as the new residents have taken possession, he should send round his card. "Tell me what is worrying you," he would say, "and I will see that something is done about it." He might charge a couple of guineas as his fee. Perhaps it would be better if he said, "Let me tell you what is likely to worry you" — if, that is to say, his business was to go round your house directly you got into it, to make a list of the jobs that wanted doing, and then, armed with your authority, to go off and get them done. Many people would gladly pay him two guineas for such excellent services, and he could probably pick up a trifle more as commission from the men to whom he gave the work. It would be worth trying anyway.

23

But, of course, such a man would have to have a vast knowledge of affairs. He would have to know, for instance, how one buys string. In the ordinary way one doesn't buy string; it comes to you, and you take it off and send it back again. But the occasion may arise when you want lots and lots of it. Then it is necessary to look for a string shop. A friend of mine spent the whole of one afternoon trying to buy a ball of string. He wandered from one ironmonger to the other (he had a fixed idea that an ironmonger was the man), and finally, in despair, went into a large furnishing shop, noted for its "artistic suites." He was very humble by this time, and his petition that they should sell him some string because he was an old customer of theirs was unfortunately worded. As far as I know he is still stringless, just as I am still waiting for somebody to do something about the cistern.

Christmas Games

The shops are putting on their Christmas dress. The cotton-wool, that time-hallowed substitute for snow, is creeping into the plate-glass windows; the pink lace collars are encircling again the cakes; and the "charming wedding or birthday present" of a week ago renews its youth as a "suitable Yuletide gift." Everything calls to us to get our Christmas shopping done early this year, but, as usual, we shall put it off until the latest possible day, and in that last mad rush we shall get Aunt Emily the wrong pair of mittens and overlook poor Uncle John altogether.

Before I begin my own shopping I am waiting for an announcement in the papers. All that my paper has told me is that the Christmas toy bazaars of the big stores are now open. I have not yet seen that list and description of the new games of the season for which I wait so eagerly. It is possible that this year will produce the masterpiece—the game which possesses in the highest degree all the qualities of the ideal Christmas game. The unfortunate thing is that, even if such a game were to appear in this year's catalogue, we should have lost it by next year; for the National Sporting Club (or whoever arranges these things) has always been convinced that "novelty" is the one quality required at Christmas, the hall-mark of excellence which no Christmas shopper can resist. If a game is novel, it is enough. To the manager of a toy department the continued vogue of cricket must be very bewildering.

Let us consider the ideal Christmas game. In the first place, it must be a round game; that is to say, at least six people must be able to play it simultaneously. No game for two only is permissible at Christmas—unless, of course, it be under the mistletoe. Secondly, it must be a game into which skill does not enter, or, if it does, it must be a skill which is as likely to be shown by a child of eight or an old gentleman of eighty as by a 'Varsity blue. Such skill, for instance, as manifests itself at Tiddleywinks, that noble game. Yet, even so,

Tiddleywinks is too skilful a pursuit. One cannot say what it is that makes a good Tiddleywinker, whether eye or wrist or supple finger-work, but it is obvious that one who is "winking" badly must be depressed by the thought that he is appearing stupid and clumsy to his neighbours, and that this feeling is not conducive to that happiness which his many Christmas cards have called down upon him.

It is better, therefore, that the element of skill should be absent. Let it be a game of luck only; and, since it is impossible to play a Christmas game for money, you will not be depressed if you lose.

The third and last essential of the ideal game is that it must provoke laughter. You cannot laugh at Tiddleywinks, nor at Ludo (as I hear, but I have never yet discovered what Ludo is), nor at Happy Families. But the ideal game is provocative of that best kind of laughter—laughter at the undeserved misfortunes of others, seasoned by the knowledge that at any moment a similar misfortune may happen to oneself.

Just before the war I came across the ideal game. I forget what it was called, unless it was some such name as "The Prince's Quest." Six princes, suitably coloured, set out to win the hand of the beautiful princess. They started at one end of a long and winding road, and she waited for the first arrival at the other end. The road, which passed through the most enthralling scenery, was numbered by milestones—"1" to "200". Suppose you were the Red Prince, you shook a die (I mean the half of two dice), and if a four turned up, you advanced to the fourth milestone. And so on, in succession. So far it doesn't sound very exciting. But you are forgetting the scenery. Perhaps at the twelfth milestone there awaited you the shoes of swiftness, which carried you in one bound to the twentieth milestone; thus by throwing a three at the ninth, you advanced eleven miles, whereas if you had thrown a four you would only have advanced four miles. On arriving at other lucky milestones you received a cloak of darkness, which took you past various obstacles which were holding the others up, or perhaps were introduced to a potent dwarf, who showed you a short cut forbidden to your rivals. One way and another you pushed ahead of the other princes.

And then the inevitable happened. You arrived at the eighty-fourth milestone (or whatever it was) and you found a wicked enchanter waiting for you, who cast upon you a backward spell, as a result of which you had to travel backwards for the next three turns. Undaunted by this reverse, you returned bravely to it, and perhaps came upon the eighty-fourth milestone again. But even so you did not despair, for there was always hope. The Blue Prince, who is now leading, approaches the ninety-sixth milestone. He is, indeed, at the ninety-fifth. A breathless moment as he shakes the die. Will he? He does. He throws a one, reaches the ninety-sixth milestone, topples headlong into the underground river, and is swept back to the starting-point again.

A great game. But our edition of it went to some hospital during the war, and I fear now that I shall never play it again. Yet I scan the papers eagerly, hoping for some announcement of it. Not this actual game, of course, but some version of it; some "Christmas novelty," in which, perhaps, the princes are called knights, but the laughter remains the same.

The Mathematical Mind

My daily paper just now is full of mathematical difficulties, submitted by its readers for the amusement of one of its staff. Every morning he appeals to us for assistance in solving tricky little problems about pints of water and herrings and rectangular fields. The magic number "9" has a great fascination for him. It is terrifying to think that if you multiply any row of figures by 9 the sum of the figures thus obtained is divisible by 9. It is uncanny to hear that if a clock takes six seconds to strike six it takes as much as thirteen seconds and a fifth to strike twelve.

As a relief from searching for news in a press devoid of news, the study of these problems is welcome enough, and to the unmathematical mind, no doubt, the solutions appear to be something miraculous. But to the mathematical mind a thing more miraculous is the awe with which the unmathematical regard the simplest manipulation of figures. Most of my life at school was spent in such pursuits that I feel bound to claim the mathematical mind to some extent, with the result that I can look down wonderingly upon these deeps of ignorance yawning daily in the papers—much, I dare say, as the senior wrangler looks down upon me. Figures may puzzle me occasionally, but at least they never cause me surprise or alarm.

Naturally, then, I am jealous for the mathematical mind. If a man who makes a false quantity, or attributes Lycidas to Keats, is generally admitted to be uncultured, I resent it very much that no stigma attaches to the gentleman who cannot do short division. I remember once at school having to do a piece of Latin prose about the Black Hole of Calcutta. It was a moving story as told in our prose book, and I had spent an interesting hour turning into fairly correct and wholly uninspired Latin—the sort of Latin I suppose which a small uneducated Roman child (who had heard the news) would have written to a school-boy friend. The size of the Black

Hole was given as "twenty foot square." I had no idea how to render this idiomatically, but I knew that a room 20 ft. square contained 400 square feet. Also I knew the Latin for one square foot. But you will not be surprised to hear that my form master, a man of culture and education, leapt upon me.

"Quadringenti," he snapped, "is 400, not 20."

"Quite so," I agreed. "The room had 400 square feet."

"Read it again. It says 20 square feet."

"No, no, 20 feet square."

He glared at me in indignation. "What's the difference?" he said.

I sighed and began to explain. I went on explaining. If there had not been other things to do than teaching cultured and educated schoolmasters, I might be explaining still.

Yes, I resented this; and I resent now the matter-of-fact way in which we accept the ignorance of mathematics shown by our present teachers—the press. At every election in which there are only two candidates a dozen papers discover with amazement this astounding coincidence in the figures: that the decrease in, say, the Liberal vote subtracted from the increase in the Conservative vote is exactly equal to the increase in the poll. If there should happen to be three candidates for a seat, the coincidences discovered are yet more numerous and astonishing. Last Christmas a paper let itself go still further, and dived into the economics of the plum pudding. A plum pudding contains raisins, flour, and sugar. Raisins had gone up 2d. a pound, or whatever it was, flour 6d., and sugar 1d. Hence the pudding now would cost 9d. a pound more!

Consider, too, the extraordinary antics of the press over the methods of scoring in the cricket championship. Wonderful new suggestions are made which, if followed, could only have the effect of bringing the teams out in exactly the same order as before. The simplest of simple problems in algebra would have shown them this, but they feared to mix themselves up with such unknown powers of darkness. The Theory of Probability, again, leaves the press entirely cold, so that it is ready to father any childish "system" for Monte Carlo. And nine men out of ten really believe that, if you toss a penny five times in the air and it comes down heads each time, it is more likely to come down tails than heads next time.

Yet papers and people who think like this are considered quite capable of dealing with the extraordinarily complicated figures of national finance. They may boom or condemn insurance bills and fiscal policies, and we listen to them reverently. As long as they know what Mr. Gladstone said in '74, it doesn't seem to matter at all what Mr. Todhunter said in his "Arithmetic for Beginners."

Going Out to Dinner

If you are one of those lucky people whose motor is not numbered (as mine is) 19 or 11 or 22, it does not really matter where your host for the evening prefers to live; Bayswater or Battersea or Blackheath—it is all the same to your chauffeur. But for those of us who have to fight for bus or train or taxicab, it is different. We have to say to ourselves, "Is it worth it?" A man who lives in Chelsea (for instance) demands more from an invitation to Hampstead than from an invitation to Kensington. If such a man were interested in people rather than in food, he might feel that one actor-manager and a rural dean among his fellow-guests would be sufficient attraction in a Kensington house, but that at least two archbishops and a revue-producer would have to be forthcoming at Hampstead before the journey on a wet night would be justified. On the other hand, if he were a vulgar man who preferred food to people, he would divide London up into whisky, burgundy, and champagne areas according to their accessibility from his own house; and on receiving an invitation to a house in the outer or champagne area (as it might be at Dulwich), he would try to discover, either by inquiry among his friends or by employing a private detective, whether this house fulfilled the necessary condition. If not, of course, then he would write a polite note to say that he would be in the country, or confined to his bed with gout, on the day in question.

I am as fond of going out to dinner as anyone else is, but there is a moment, just before I begin to array myself for it, when I wish that it were on some other evening. If the telephone bell rings, I say, "Thank Heavens, Mrs. Parkinson-Jones has died suddenly. I mean, how sad," and, looking as solemn as I can, I pick up the receiver.

"Is that the Excelsior Laundry?" says a voice. "You only sent back half a pair of socks this week."

I replace the receiver and go reluctantly upstairs to dress. There is

31

no help for it. As I dress, I wonder who my partner at the table will be, and if at this moment she is feeling as gloomy about the prospects as I am. How much better if we had both dined comfortably at home. I remember some years ago taking in a Dowager Countess. Don't think that I am priding myself on this; I realize as well as you do that a mistake of some sort was made. Probably my hostess took me for somebody else—Sir Thomas Lipton, it may have been. Anyway the Dowager Countess and I led the way downstairs to the dining-room, and all the other guests murmured to themselves, "Who on earth is that?" and told each other that no doubt I was one of the Serbian Princes who had recently arrived in the country. I forgot what the Countess and I talked about; probably yachts, or tea; but I was not paying much attention to our conversation. I had other things to think about.

For the Dowager Countess (wisely, I think) was dieting herself. She went through the evening on a glass of water and two biscuits. Each new dish on its way round the table was brought first to her; she waved it away, and it came to me. There was nothing to be done. I had to open it.

My particular memory is of a quail-pie. Quails may be all right for Moses in the desert, but, if they are served in the form of pie at dinner, they should be distributed at a side-table, not handed round from guest to guest. The Countess having shuddered at it and resumed her biscuit, it was left to me to make the opening excavation. The difficulty was to know where each quail began and ended; the job really wanted a professional quail-finder, who might have indicated the point on the surface of the crust at which it would be most hopeful to dig for quails.

As it was, I had to dig at random, and, being unlucky, I plunged the knife straight into the middle of a bird. It was impossible, of course, to withdraw the quail through the slit I had thus made in the pastry, nor could I get my knife out (with a bird sticking on the end of it) in order to make a second slit at a suitable angle. I tried to shake the quail off inside the pie, but it was fixed too firmly. I tried

32

pulling it off against the inside of the crust, but it became obvious that if I persisted in this, the whole roof would come off. The footman, with great presence of mind, realized my difficulty and offered me a second knife. Unfortunately, I misjudged the width of quails, and plunging this second knife into the pie a little farther on, I landed into the middle of another quail no less retentive of cutlery than the first. The dish now began to look more like a game than a pie, and, waving away a third knife, I said (quite truly by this time) that I didn't like quails, and that on second thoughts I would ask the Dowager Countess to lend me a biscuit.

Fortunately, dinner is not all quail-pie. But even in the case of some more amenable dish, the first-comer is in a position of great responsibility. Casting a hasty eye round the company, he has to count the number of diners, estimate the size of the dish, divide the one by the other, and take a helping of the appropriate size, knowing that the fashion which he inaugurates will be faithfully followed. How much less exacting is the position of the more lowly-placed man; my own, for instance, on ordinary occasions. There may be two quails and an egg-cup left when the footman reaches me, or even only the egg-cup, but at least I have nobody but myself to consider.

But let us get away from food for the body, and consider food for the mind. I refer to that intellectual conversation which it is the business of the guests at a dinner-party to contribute. Not "What shall we eat?" but "What shall be talk about?" is the question which is really disturbing us as we tug definitely at our necktie and give a last look at ourselves in the glass before following the servant upstairs.

"Will you take in Miss Montmorency?" says our hostess.

We bow to Miss Montmorency hopefully.

"Er—jolly day it's been, hasn't it?"

No, really, we can't say anything about the weather. We must be original.

"Er—have you been to any theatres lately?"

No, no, everybody says that. Well, then, what can we say? Let us try again.

"How do you do. Er—I see by the paper this evening that the Bolsheviks have captured Omsk."

"Captured Whatsk?"

"Omsk." Or was it Tomsk? Fortunately it does not matter, for Miss Montmorency is not the least interested.

"Oh!" she says.

I hate people who say "Oh!" It means that you have to begin all over again.

"I've been playing golfsk—I mean golf—this afternoon," we try. "Do you play at all?"

"No."

Then it is no good telling her what our handicap is.

"No doubt your prefer tennis," we hazard.

"Oh no."

"I mean bridge."

"I don't play any game," she answers.

Then the sooner she goes away and talks to somebody else the better.

"Ah, I expect you're more interested in the theatre?"

"I hardly ever go to the theatre."

"Well, of course, a good book by the fireside—"

34

"I never read," she says.

Dash the woman, what does she do? But before we can ask her, she lets us into the great secret.

"I like talking," she says.

Good Heavens! What else have we been trying to do all this time?

However, it is only the very young girl at her first dinner-party whom it is difficult to entertain. At her second dinner-party, and thereafter, she knows the whole art of being amusing. All she has to do is to listen; all we men have to do is to tell her about ourselves. Indeed, sometimes I think that it is just as well to begin at once. Let us be quite frank about it, and get to work as soon as we are introduced.

"How do you do. Lovely day it has been, hasn't it? It was on just such a day as this, thirty-five years ago, that I was born in the secluded village of Puddlecome of humble but honest parents. Nestling among the western hills..."

And so on. Ending, at the dessert, with the thousand we earned that morning.

The Etiquette of Escape

There is a girl in one of William de Morgan's books who interrupts the narrator of a breathless tiger-hunting story with the rather disconcerting warning, "I'm on the side of the tiger; I always am." It was the sporting instinct. Tigers may be wicked beasts who defend themselves when they are attacked, but one cannot help feeling a little sorry for them. Their number is up. The hunters are too many, the rifles too accurate, for the hunted to have any real chance. So she was on the side of the tiger; she always was.

In the same way I am on the side of the convict; I always am. Not, of course, until he is a convict. But when once the Law has condemned him, and he is safely in prison, then he is only one against so many. It is impossible not to sympathize with his attempts to escape. Perhaps, if one lived close to a prison, in a cottage, say, whose tenant was invariably called upon by any escaping prisoner and made to exchange clothes with the help of a crow-bar, one might feel differently. But in theory we are all of us inclined to applaud the man who fights successfully such a lone battle against such tremendous odds; yes, even if it was the blackest of crimes which sent him into captivity.

It is, therefore, extraordinarily jolly to read about the escape of political prisoners from gaol. One has to stifle no protests from one's conscience while applauding them, for it is absurd to suppose that the world is any the worse place for their being loose again. Probably they are much more dangerous in prison than out of it. But besides applauding them, one envies them heartily. What fun they must have had when arranging it! What fun, too, to attempt an escape, when the worst that can happen to you, if you are recaptured, is that the next escape becomes a little more difficult. No bread and water, no punishment cell for a political prisoner.

All the same, these are not quite the ideal escapes. I am a trifle exigent in such matters. I allow my prisoners a little latitude, but there are certain rules which must be observed. Sinn Feiners, for instance, make it much too easy for themselves. Their friends from outside are permitted to visit them, and to discuss openly (but of course, in Irish) all the arrangements for the great day. When the day comes, they make off by motor-car, and as likely as not have a steam-yacht waiting for them on the coast. It was not thus that I used to escape in the early nineties. I observed the rules.

The first rule was that the only means of communication with outside was the roll of bread which formed one's principal meal. Biting eagerly into the bread, the hungry prisoner found himself entangled in a message from his loved one. Of course, in these last few years he would just have thought that it was part of the bread, perhaps a trifle more indigestible than usual, but in those days he would have no excuse for not realizing that his Araminta was getting into touch with him. This first message did not say much; just "All my love, and I am sending a file to-morrow," so as to prevent him from breaking his jaw on it. On the next day, he would open the roll cautiously, and behold! a small file would be embedded within.

It is wonderful what can be done with quite a small file. But we must remember that the world moved more slowly in those days. One had leisure in which to do a job of work properly. Perhaps our prisoner took a couple of years filing the gyves off his wrists (holding the file carefully in the teeth), and another year to remove the manacles from his ankles. Fortunately he was left alone to pursue these avocations. The goaler pushed in the daily portion of bread and water, but made no inquiry about his prisoner's well-being. Only the essential tame rat kept him company, and Araminta outside, to whom he dropped an occasional note to say that he had done another millimetre that morning. Perhaps she did not get it; it was borne swiftly away by the river which flowed beneath the walls, and never came to the opposite bank, whereon she waited for him. But she did not lose hope. These things always took a long time.

And then, when the fetters had been removed, and two of the bars in the narrow window had been sawn through, there came the great moment. The prisoner was now free to tear his sheet and his blanket and his underclothes into strips, and plait himself a rope. One had to time this for the summer, of course. One couldn't go cutting up one's shirt in the middle of winter. So, upon a dark night in August, the prisoner tied his rope to the remaining bar, squeezed through the window, and let himself down into space. Was the rope long enough? It wasn't, of course; it never was. But, once at the end of it, the prisoner would realize, his senses quickened by the emergency, that it was too late to go back. From the extreme end he breathed a prayer and dropped.... Splash! And five minutes later he was embracing Araminta. There was no pursuit; they were sportsmen in those days, and it was recognized that he had won.

That is the classic mode of escape. But there are variants of it which I am prepared to allow. The goaler may have a daughter, who, moved by the romantic history and pallor of the prisoner, may exchange clothes with him. The prisoner may pass himself off for dead, may be actually buried, and then rescued from the grave just in time by the pre-warned and ever-ready Araminta. There are many legitimate ways of escape, but the essential thing is that all messages to the prisoner from his Araminta outside should be conveyed in his loaf of bread. To whisper them in Irish is too easy, too unromantic.

But in any case I am on the side of the prisoner. I always am.

Geographical Research

The other day I met a man who didn't know where Tripoli was. Tripoli happened to come into the conversation, and he was evidently at a loss. "Let's see," he said. "Tripoli is just down by the—er—you know. What's the name of that place?" "That's right," I answered, "just opposite Thingumabob. I could show you in a minute on the map. It's near—what do they call it?" At this moment the train stopped, and I got out and went straight home to look at my atlas.

Of course I really knew exactly where Tripoli was. About thirty years ago, when I learnt geography, one of the questions they were always asking me was, "What are the exports of Spain, and where is Tripoli?" But much may happen in twenty years; coast erosion and tidal waves and things like that. I looked at the map in order to assure myself that Tripoli had remained pretty firm. As far as I could make it out it had moved. Certainly it must have looked different thirty years ago, for I took some little time to locate it. But no doubt one's point of view changes with the decades. To a boy Tripoli might seem a long way from Italy—even in Asia Minor; but when he grew up his standards of measurement would be altered. Tripoli would appear in its proper place due south of Sicily.

I always enjoy these periodic excursions to my atlas. People talk a good deal of nonsense about the importance of teaching geography at school instead of useless subjects like Latin and Greek, but so long as you have an atlas near you, of what use is geography? Why waste time learning where Tripoli and Fiume are, when you can turn to a map of Africa and spot them in a moment? In a leading article in The Times (no less—our premier English newspaper) it was stated during a general election that Darlington was in Yorkshire. You may say that The Times leader writers ought to have been taught geography; I say that unfortunately they have been taught geography. They learnt, or thought they learnt, that

Darlington was a Yorkshire town. If they had been left in a state of decent ignorance, they would have looked for Darlington in the map and found that it was in Durham. (One moment—Map 29— Yes, Durham; that's right.) As it is, there are at this moment some hundreds of retired colonels who go about believing implicitly that Darlington is in Yorkshire because The Times has said it. How much more important than a knowledge of geography is the possession of an atlas.

My own atlas is a particularly fine specimen. It contains all sorts of surprising maps which never come into ordinary geography. I think my favourite is a picture of the Pacific Ocean, coloured in varying shades of blue according to the depths of the sea. The deep ultramarine terrifies me. I tremble for a ship which is passing over it, and only breathe again when it reaches the very palest blue. There is one little patch—the Nero Deep in the Ladrone Basin— which is actually 31,614 feet deep. I suppose if you sailed over it you would find it no bluer than the rest of the sea, and if you fell into it you would feel no more alarmed than if it were 31,613 feet deep; but still you cannot see it in the atlas without a moment's awe.

Then my atlas has a map of "The British Empire showing the great commercial highways"; another of "The North Polar regions showing the progress of explorations"; maps of the trade routes, of gulf streams, and beautiful things of that kind. It tells you how far it is from Southampton to Fremantle, so that if you are interested in the M.C.C. Australian team you can follow them day by day across the sea. Why, with all your geographical knowledge you couldn't even tell me the distance between Yokohama and Honolulu, but I can give the answer in a moment—3,379 miles. Also I know exactly what a section of the world along lat. 45 deg. N. looks like—and there are very few of our most learned men who can say as much.

But my atlas goes even farther than this, though I for one do not follow it. It gives diagrams of exports and imports; it tells you where things are manufactured or where grown; it gives pictures of sheep—an immense sheep representing New Zealand and a mere insect representing Russia, and alas! no sheep at all for Canada and Germany and China. Then there are large cigars for America and small mild cigars for France and Germany; pictures in colour of such unfamiliar objects as spindles and raw silk and miners and Mongolians and iron ore; statistics of traffic receipts and diamonds. I say that I don't follow my atlas here, because information of this sort does not seem to belong properly to an atlas. This is not my idea of geography at all. When I open my atlas I open it to look at maps—to find out where Tripoli is—not to acquire information about flax and things; yet I cannot forego the boast that if I wanted I could even speak at length about flax.

And lastly there is the index. Running my eye down it, I can tell you in less than a minute where such different places as Jorobado, Kabba, Hidegkut, Paloo, and Pago Pago are to be found. Could you, even after your first-class honours in the Geography Tripos, be as certain as I am? Of Hidegkut, perhaps, or Jorobado, but not of Pago Pago.

On the other hand, you might possibly have known where Tripoli was.

Children's Plays

At the beginning of every pantomime season, we are brought up against two original discoveries. The first is that Mr. Arthur Collins has undoubtedly surpassed himself; the other, that "the children's pantomime" is not really a pantomime for children at all. Mr. Collins, in fact, has again surpassed himself in providing an entertainment for men and women of the world.

One has to ask oneself, then, what sort of pantomime children really like. I ought to know, because I once tried to write one, and some kind critic was found to say (as generally happens on these occasions) that I showed "a wonderful insight into the child's mind." Perhaps he was thinking of the elephant. The manager had a property elephant left over from some other play which he had produced lately. There it was, lying in the wings and getting in everybody's way. I think he had left it about in the hope that I might be inspired by it. At one of the final rehearsals, after I had fallen over this elephant several times, he said, "It's a pity we aren't going to use the elephant. Couldn't you get it in somewhere?" I said that I thought I could. After all, getting an elephant into a play is merely a question of stagecraft. If you cannot get an elephant on and off the stage in a natural way, your technique is simply hopeless, and you had better give up writing plays altogether. I need hardly say that my technique was quite up to the work. At the critical moment the boy-hero said, "Look, there's an elephant," pointing to that particular part of the stage by which alone it could enter, and there, sure enough, the elephant was. It then went through its trick of conveying a bun to its mouth, after which the boy said, "Good-bye, elephant," and it was hauled off backwards. Of course it intruded a certain gross materialism into the delicate fancy of my play, but I did not care to say so, because one has to keep in with the manager. Besides, there was the elephant, eating its head off; it might just as well be used.

Well, so far as the children were concerned, the elephant was the success of the play. Up to the moment of its entrance they were—well, I hope not bored, but no more than politely interested. But as soon as the hero said, "Look, there's an elephant," you could feel them all jumping up and down in their seats and saying "Oo!" Nor was this "Oo" atmosphere ever quite dispelled thereafter. The elephant had withdrawn, but there was always the hope now that he might come on again, and if an elephant, why not a giraffe, a hippopotamus, or a polar-bear? For the rest of the pantomime every word was followed with breathless interest. At any moment the hero might come out with another brilliant line—"Look, there's a hippopotamus." Even when it was proved, with the falling of the final curtain, that the author had never again risen to these heights, there was still one chance left. Perhaps if they clapped loudly enough, the elephant would hear, and would take a call like the others.

What sort of pantomime do children like? It is a strange thing that we never ask ourselves "What sort of plays—or books or pictures—do public-school men like?" You say that that would be an absurd question. Yet it is not nearly so absurd as the other. For the real differences of thought and feeling between you and your neighbour were there when you were children, and your agreements are the result of the subsequent community of interests which you have shared—in similar public-schools, universities, services, or professions. Why should two children want to see the same pantomime? Apart from the fact that "two children" may mean such different samples of humanity as a boy of five and a girl of fifteen, is there any reason why Smith's child and Robinson's child should think alike? And as for your child, my dear sir (or madam), I have only to look at it—and at you—to see at once how utterly different it is from every other child which has ever been born. Obviously it would want something very much superior to the sort of pantomime which would amuse those very ordinary children of which Smith and Robinson are so proud.

I cannot, therefore, advance my own childish recollections of my first pantomime as trustworthy evidence of what other children like. But I should wish you to know that when I was taken to Beauty and the Beast at the age of seven, it was no elephant, nor any other kind of beast, which made the afternoon sacred for me. It was Beauty. I just gazed and gazed at Beauty. Never had I seen anything so lovely. For weeks afterwards I dreamed about her. Nothing that was said or done on the stage mattered so long as she was there. Probably the author had put some of his most delightful work into that pantomime—"dialogue which showed a wonderful insight into the child's mind"; I apologize to him for not having listened to it. (I can sympathize with him now.) Or it may be that the author had written for men and women of the world; his dialogue was full of that sordid cynicism about married life which is still considered amusing, so that the aunt who took me wondered if this were really a pantomime suitable for children. Poor dear!—as if I heard a word of it, I who was just waiting for Beauty to come back.

What do children like? I do not think that there is any answer to that question. They like anything; they like everything; they like so many different things. But I am certain that there has never been an ideal play for very young children. It will never be written, for the reason that no self-respecting writer could bore himself so completely as to write it. (Also it is doubtful if fathers and mothers, uncles and aunts, would sacrifice themselves a second time, after they had once sat through it.) For very young children do not want humour or whimsicality or delicate fancy or any of the delightful properties which we attribute to the ideal children's play. I do not say that they will rise from their stalls and call loudly for their perambulators, if these qualities creep into the play, but they can get on very happily without them. All that they want is a continuous procession of ordinary everyday events—the arrival of elephants (such as they see at the Zoo), or of postmen and policemen (such as they see in their street), the simplest form of clowning or of practical joke, the most photographically dull dialogue. For a grown-up it would be an appalling play to sit through, and still more appalling play to have to write.

44

Perhaps you protest that your children love Peter Pan. Of course they do. They would be horrible children if they didn't. And they would be horrible children if they did not love (as I am sure they do) a Drury Lane pantomime. A nice child would love Hamlet. But I also love Peter Pan; and for this reason I feel that it cannot possibly be the ideal play for children. I do not, however, love the Drury Lane pantomime... which leaves me with the feeling that it may really be "the children's pantomime" after all.

The Road to Knowledge

My pipe being indubitably smoked out to the last grain, I put it in my pocket and went slowly up to the nursery, trying to feel as much like that impersonation of a bear which would inevitably be demanded of me as is possible to a man of mild temperament. But I had alarmed myself unnecessarily. There was no demand for bears. Each child lay on its front, engrossed in a volume of The Children's Encyclopaedia. Nobody looked up as I came in. Greatly relieved, I also took a volume of the great work and lay down on my front. I came away from my week-end a different man. For the first time in my life I was well informed. If you had only met me on the Monday and asked me the right questions, I could have surprised you. Perhaps, even now... but alas! my knowledge is slipping away from me, and probably the last of it will be gone before I have finished this article.

For this Encyclopaedia (as you may have read in the advertisements) makes a feature of answering all those difficult questions which children ask grown-ups, and which grown-ups really want to ask somebody else. Well, perhaps not all those questions. There are two to which there were no answers in my volume, nor, I suspect, in any of the other volumes, and yet these are the two questions more often asked than any others. "How did God begin?" and "Where do babies come from?" Perhaps they were omitted because the answers to them are so easy. "That, my child, is something which you had better ask your mother," one replies; or if one is the mother, "You must wait till you are grown-up, dear." Nor did I see any mention of the most difficult question of all, the question of the little girl who had just been assured that God could do anything. "Then, if He can do anything, can He make a stone so heavy that He can't lift it?" Perhaps the editor is waiting for his second edition before he answers that one. But upon such matters as "Why does a stone sink?" or "Where does the wind come from?" or "What makes thunder?" he is delightfully informing.

But I felt all the time that in this part of his book he really had his eye on me and my generation rather than on the children. No child wants to know why a stone sinks; it knows the answer already— "What else could it do?" Even Sir Isaac Newton was a grown-up before he asked why an apple fell, and there had been men in the world fifty thousand years before that (yes I have been reading The Outline of History, too), none of whom bothered his head about gravitation. Yes, the editor was thinking all the time that you and I ought to know more about these things. Of course, we should be too shy to order the book for ourselves, but we could borrow it from our young friends occasionally on the plea of seeing if it was suitable for them, and so pick up a little of that general knowledge which we lack so sadly. Where does the wind come from? Well, really, I don't think I know now.

The drawback of all Guides to Knowledge is that one cannot have the editor at hand in order to cross-examine him. This is particularly so in the case of a Children's Encyclopaedia, for the child's first question, "Why does this do that?" is meant to have no more finality than tossing-up at cricket or dealing the cards at bridge. The child does not really want to know, but it does want to keep up a friendly conversation, or, if humourously inclined, to see how long you can go on without getting annoyed. Not always, of course; sometimes it really is interested; but in most cases, I suspect, the question, "What makes thunder?" is inspired by politeness or mischief. The grown-up is bursting to explain, and ought to be humoured; or else he obviously doesn't know, and ought to be shown up.

But these would not be my motives if the editor of The Children's Encyclopaedia took me for a walk and allowed me to ask him questions. The fact that light travels at so many hundred thousand miles an hour does not interest me; I should accept the information and then ask him my next question, "How did they find out?" That is always the intriguing part of the business. Who first realized that light was not instantaneous? What put him up to it? How did he measure its velocity? The fact (to take another case) that a cricket chirps by rubbing his knees together does not interest me; I want to know why he chirps. Is it involuntary, or is it done with the idea of pleasing? Why does a bird sing? The editor is prepared to tell me why a parrot is able to talk, but that is a much less intriguing matter. Why does a bird sing? I do not want an explanation of a thrush's song or a nightingale's, but why does a silly bird go on saying "chiff-chaff" all day long? Is it, for instance, happiness or hiccups?

Possibly these things are explained in some other volume than the one which fell to me. Possibly they are inexplicable. We can dogmatize about a star a billion miles away, but we cannot say with certainty how an idea came to a man or a song to a bird. Indeed, I think, perhaps, it would have been wiser of me to have left the chiff-chaff out of it altogether. I have an uneasy feeling that all last year the chiff-chaff was asking himself why I wrote every day. Was it involuntary, he wondered, or was it done with the idea of pleasing?

A Man of Property

Yes, a gardener's life is a disappointing one. When it was announced that we were just too late for everything this year, I decided to buy some ready-made gardens and keep them about the house, until such time as Nature was ready to co-operate. So now I have three gardens. This enables me to wear that superior look (which is so annoying for you) when you talk about your one little garden in front of me. Then you get off in disgust and shoot yourself, and they bury you in what you proudly called your herbaceous border, and people wonder next year why the delphiniums are so luxuriant—but you are not there to tell them.

Yes, I have three gardens. You come upon the first one as you are shown up the staircase to the drawing-room. It is outside the staircase window. This is the daffodil garden—3 ft. 8 ins. by 9 ins. The vulgar speak of it as a window-box; that is how one knows that they are vulgar. The maid has her instructions; we are not at home when next they call.

Sometimes I sit on the stairs and count the daffodils in my garden. There are seventy-eight of them; seventy-eight or seventy-nine—I cannot say for certain, because they will keep nodding their heads, so that sometimes one may escape me, or perhaps I may count another one twice over. The wall round the daffodil garden is bright blue—I painted it myself, and still carry patterns of it about with me—and the result of all these yellow heads on their long green necks waving above the blue walls of my garden is that we are always making excuses to each other for going up and down stairs, and the bell in the drawing-room is never rung.

But I have a fault to find with my daffodils. They turn their backs on us. It is natural, I suppose, that they do not care to look in at the window to see what we are doing, preferring the blue sky and the sun, and all that they can catch of March and April, but the end of it is that we see too little of their faces; for even if they are trained in youth with a disposition towards the window, yet as soon as they begin to come to their full glory they swing round towards the south and hide their beauty from us. But the House Opposite sees them, and brings his visitors, you may be sure, to his window to look at them. Indeed, I should not be surprised if he boasted of it as "his garden" and were even now writing in a book about it.

My second garden is circular—18 ins. in diameter, and, of course, more than that all the way round. I can see it now as I write—or, more accurately, if I stop writing for a moment—for it is just outside the library window. The vulgar call it a tub—they would; actually it is the Tulip Garden. At least, the man says so. For the tulips have not bourgeoned yet. No, I am wrong. (That is the worst of using these difficult words.) They have bourgeoned, but they have not blossomed. Their heads are well above ground, they have swelled into buds, but the buds have not broken. So, for all I know, they may yet be sun-flowers. However, the man says they will be tulips; he was paid for tulips; and he assures me that he has had experience in these matters. For myself, I should never dare to speak with so much authority. It is not our birth but our upbringing which makes us what we are, and these tulips have had, during their short lives above ground, a fatherly care and a watchfulness neither greater nor less than were bestowed upon the daffodils. That they sprang from different bulbs seems to me a small matter in comparison with this. However, the man says that they will be tulips. Presumably yellow ones.

One's gardens get smaller and smaller. My third is only 11 ins. by 9 ins. The vulgar call it a Japanese garden—indeed, I don't see what else they could call it. East is East and West is West and never the twain shall meet, but this does not prevent my Japanese garden from sitting on an old English refectory table in the dining-room. A Japanese garden needs very careful management. I have three native gardeners working at it day and night. At least they maintain the attitudes of men hard at work, but they don't seem to do much; perhaps they are afraid of throwing one another out of employment. The head gardener spends his time pointing to the largest cactus, and saying (I suppose in Japanese), "Look at my cactus!" The other two appear to be washing his Sunday shirt for him, instead of pruning or potting out, which is what I pay them for. However, the whole scene is one of great activity, for in the ornamental water in the middle of the garden two fishermen are hard at it, hoping to land something for my breakfast. So far they have not had a bite.

My Japanese garden has this advantage over the others, that it is independent of the seasons. The daffodils will bow their heads and droop away. The tulips—well, let us be sure that they are tulips first; but, if the man is correct, they too will wither. But the green hedgehog which friends tell me is a cactus will just go on and on. It must have some source of self-nourishment, for it can derive little from the sand whereon it rests. Perhaps, like most of us, it thrives on appreciation, and the gardener, who points to it so proudly day and night, is rightly employed after all. He knows that if once he dropped his hand, or looked the other way, the cactus would give it up disheartened.

It is fortunate for you that I am writing this week, and not later, for I have now ordered three more gardens, circular ones, to sit outside the library. There is talk also of a couple of evergreen woods for the front of the house. With six gardens, two woods, and an ornamental lake I shall be unbearable. In all the gardens of England people will be shooting themselves in disgust, and the herbaceous borders will flourish as never before. But that is for the future. To-day I write only of my three gardens. I would write of them at greater length but that my daffodil garden is sending out an irresistible call. I go to sit on the staircase.

An Ordnance Map

Spring calls to us to be up and about. It shouts to us to stand bareheaded upon hills and look down upon little woods and tiny red cottages, and away up to where the pines stand straight into the sky. Let the road, thin and white, wander on alone; we shall meet it again, and it shall lead us if it will to some comfortable inn; but now we are for the footpath and the stile—we are to stand in the fields and listen to the skylark.

Must you stay and work in London? But you will have ten minutes to spare. Look, I have an ordnance map—let us take our walk upon that.

We will start, if you please, at Buckley Cross. That is the best of walking on the map; you may start where you like, and there are no trains to catch. Our road goes north through the village—shall we stop a moment to buy an apple or two? Apples go well in the open air; we shall sit upon a gate presently and eat them before we light our pipes and join the road again. A pound, if you will—and now with bulging pockets for the north.

Over Buckley Common. You see by the dotted lines that it is an unfenced road, as, indeed, it should be over gorse and heather. A mile of it, and then it branches into two. Let us take this lane on the left; the way seems more wooded to the west.

By now we should be passing Buckley Grove. Perhaps it is for sale. If so, we might stop for a minute or two and buy it. We can work out how many acres it is, because it is about three-quarters of an inch each way, and if we could only remember how many acres went to a square mile—well, anyhow, it is a good-sized place. But three miles from a station, you say? Ah yes, but look at that little mark there just round the corner. Do you know what that stands for? A wind pump. How jolly to have one at your very door. "Shall we go and look at the wind pump?" you would say casually to your guests.

Let us leave the road. Do you see those dots going off to the right? That is a footpath. I have an idea that that will take us to the skylark. They do not mark skylarks on the map—I cannot say why—but something tells me that about a mile farther on, where the dots begin to bend.... Ah, do you hear? Up and up and up he goes into the blue, fainter and fainter falls the music. He calls to us to follow him to the clean morning of the world, whose magic light has shone for us in our dreams so long, yet ever eluded us waking. Bathed in that light, Youth is not so young as we, nor Beauty more beautiful; in that light Happiness is ours at last, for Endeavour shall have its perfect fulfilment, a fulfilment without regret....

Yes, let us have an apple.

Our path seems to end suddenly here. We shall have to go through this farm. All the dogs barking, all the fowls cluttering, all the lambs galloping—what a jolly, friendly commotion we've made! But we can get into the road again this way. Indeed, we must get into the road soon because it is hungry work out in the air, and two inches to the north-west is written a word full of meaning—the most purposeful word that can be written upon a map. "Inn," So now for a steady climb. We have dropped down to "200" by the farmhouse, and the inn is marked "500." But it is only two miles— well, barely that. Come along.

What shall we have? Ought it not to be bread and cheese and beer? But if you will excuse me, I would rather not have beer. I know that it sounds well to ask for it—as far as that goes, I will ask for it willingly—but I have never been able to drink it in any comfort. I think I shall have a gin and ginger. That also sounds well. More important still, it drinks well; in fact, the only thing which I don't like about it is the gin. "Oh, good morning. We want some bread and cheese, please, and one pint of beer, and a gin and ginger. And—er—you might leave out the gin." Yes, of course, I could have asked straight off for a plain ginger beer, but that sounds so very mild. My way I use the word "gin" twice. Let us be dashing on this brave day.

After lunch a pipe, while we consider where to go next.

It is anywhere you like, you know. To the north there is Greymoor Wood, and we pass a windmill; and to the east there is the little village of Colesford which has a church without a steeple; and to the west we go quite near another wind pump; and to the south— well, we should have to cross the line pretty soon. That brings us into touch with civilization; we do not want that just yet. So the north again let it be....

This is Greymoor Wood. Yes; there is a footpath marked right through it, but footpaths are hard to see beneath such a carpet of dead leaves. I dare say we shall lose ourselves. One false step and we are off the line of dots. There you are, there's a dot missing. We have lost the track. Now we must get out as best we can.

Do you know the way of telling the north by the sun? You turn the hour hand of your watch to the sun, and half-way between that and the XII is the south. Or else you turn the XII to the sun and take half-way between that and the hour hand. Anyhow you do find the south eventually after one or two experiments, and having discovered the south it is easy enough to locate the north. With your permission then we will push due north through Greymoor Wood.

We are through and on the road, but it is getting late. I et us hurry on. It would be tempting to wander down to that stream and follow its banks for a little; it would be pleasant to turn into that "unmetalled, unfenced" road—ah, doesn't one know those roads?—and let it carry us to the village of Milden, rich in both telegraph office and steeple. There is also, no more than two miles from where we stand, a contour of 600 ft.—shall we make for the view at the top of that? But no, perhaps you are right. We had best be getting home now. It is growing chilly; the sun has gone in; if we lost ourselves again, we could never find the north. Let us make for the nearest station. Widdington, isn't it? Three miles away....

There! Now we're home again. And must you really get on with your work? Well, but it has been a jolly day, hasn't it?

The Lord Mayor

There is a story of a boy who was asked to name ten animals which inhabit the polar regions. After a little thought he answered, "Six penguins and four seals." In the same way I suspect that, if you were asked to give the names of any three Lord Mayors of London, you would say, "Dick Whittington, and—er—Dick Whittington, and of course—er—Dick Whittington," knowing that he held that high office three times, and being quite unable to think of anybody else. This is where I have the advantage of you. In my youth there was a joke which went like this: "Why does the Lord Mayor like pepper? Because without his K.N., he'd be ill." I have an unfortunate habit of remembering even the worst joke, and so I can tell you, all these years after, that there was once a Lord Mayor called Knill. It is because I know the names of four Lord Mayors that I can write with such authority upon the subject.

To be a successful Lord Mayor demands years of training. Fortunately, the aspiring apprentice has time for preparation. From the moment when he is first elected a member of the Worshipful Company of Linendrapers he can see it coming. He can say with confidence that in 1944—or '43, if old Sir Joshua has his stroke next year, as seems probable—he will become the first citizen of London; which gives him twenty-four years in which to acquire the manner. It would be more interesting if this were not so; it would be more interesting to you and me if there were something of a struggle each year for the Lord Mayorality, so that we could put our money on our respective fancies. If, towards the end of October, we could read the Haberdashers' nominee had been for a stripped gallop on Hackney Downs and had pulled up sweating badly; if the Mayor could send a late wire from Aldgate to tell us that the candidate from the Drysalters' stable was refusing his turtle soup; if we could all try our luck at spotting the winner for November 9, then it is possible that the name of the new Lord Mayor might be as familiar in our mouths as that of this year's Derby favourite. As it is, there is no excitement at all about the business. We are told casually in a corner of the paper that Sir Tuttlebury Tupkins is to be the next Lord Mayor, and we gather that it was inevitable. The name conveys nothing to us, the face is the habitual face. He duly becomes Lord Mayor and loses his identity. We can still only think of Dick Whittington.

One cannot help wondering if it is worth it. He has his crowded year of glorious life, but it is a year without a name. He is never himself, he is just the Lord Mayor. He meets all the great people of the day, soldiers, sailors, statesmen, even artists, but they would never recognize him again. He cannot say that he knows them, even though he has given them the freedom of the City or a jewelled sword. He can do nothing to make his year of office memorable; nothing that is, which his predecessor did not do before, or his successor will not do again. If he raises a Mansion House Fund for the survivors of a flood, his predecessor had an earthquake, and his successor is safe for a famine. And nobody will remember whether it was in this year or in Sir Joshua Potts' that the record was beaten.

For this one year of anonymous greatness the aspiring Lord Mayor has to sacrifice his whole personality. He is to be the first citizen of London, but he must be very careful that London has never heard of him before. He has to live the life of a hermit, resolute neither to know nor to be known. For a year he shakes hands mechanically, but in the years before and the years afterwards, nobody, I imagine, has ever smacked him on the back. Indeed, it is doubtful if anybody has even seen him, so remote is his life from ours. He was dedicated to this from birth, or anyhow from the moment when he was first elected a member of the Worshipful Company of Linendrapers, and he has been preparing that wooden expression ever since.

It is because he has had to spend so many years out of the world that a City Remembrancer is provided for him. The City Remembrancer stands at his elbow when he receives his guests and tells him who they are. Without this aid, how should he know? Perhaps it is Mr. Thomas Hardy who is arriving. "Mr. Thomas Hardy," says the gentleman with the voice, and the Lord Mayor holds out his hand.

"I am very glad," he says, "to welcome such a very well-known—h'm—such a distinguished—er——"

"Writer," says the City Remembrancer behind the hack of his hand.

"Such a distinguished writer. The author of so many famous biog—"

"Novels," breathes the City Remembrancer, gazing up at the ceiling.

"So many famous novels," continues the Lord Mayor quite undisturbed, for he is used to it by this time. "The author of East Lynne——"

The City Remembrancer coughs and walks across to the other side of the Lord Mayor, murmuring Tess of the D'Urbervilles to the back of the Mayoral head as he goes. The Lord Mayor then repeats that he is delighted to welcome the author of Death and the Door-bells to the City, and holds out his hand to Mr. John Sargent.

"The painter," says the City Remembrancer, his lips, from long practice, hardly moving.

In the sanctity of the home that evening, while removing his chains of office, the Lord Mayor (we may suppose) tells his sleepy wife what an interesting day he has had, and how Mr. Thomas Sargent, the famous statesman, and Mr. John Hardy, the sculptor, both came to lunch.

And all the time the year is creeping on. Another day gone. Another day nearer to that fatal November 8.... And here, inevitably, is November 8, and by to-morrow he will be that most pathetic of all living creatures, an ex-Lord Mayor of London. Where do they live, the ex-Lord Mayors? They must have a colony of their own somewhere, a Garden City in which they can live together as equals. Probably they have some arrangement by which they take it in turns to be reminiscent; Sir Tuttlebury Tupkins has "and

Wednesdays" on his card, and Sir Joshua Potts receives on "3rd Mondays"; and the other Lord Mayors gather round and listen, nodding their heads. On their birthdays they give each other gold caskets, and every November 10 they march in a body to the station to welcome the new arrival. Poor fellow, the tears are streaming down his cheeks, and his paunch is shaken with sobs, but there is a hot bowl of turtle soup waiting for him at Lady Tupkins' house, The Mansion Cottage, and he will soon feel more comfortable. He has been allotted the "4th Fridays," and it is hoped that by Christmas he will have settled down quite happily at Ichabod Lodge.

The Holiday Problem

The time for a summer holiday is May, June. July, August, and September—with, perhaps a fortnight in October if the weather holds up. But it is difficult to cram all this into the few short weeks allowed to most of us. We are faced accordingly with the business of singling out one month from the others—a business invidious enough to a lover of the country, but still more so to one who loves London as well. The question for him is not only which month is most wonderful by the sea, but also which month is most tolerable out of town.

I would wash my hands of London in May and come back brown from cricket and golf and sailing in September with willingness. Alas I it is impossible. But if I pick out July as the month for the open-air life, I begin immediately to think of the superiority of July over June as a month to spend in London. Not but what June is a delightful month in town, and May and August for that matter. In May, for instance——

Let us go into this question. May, of course, is hopeless for a holiday. One must be near one's tailor in May to see about one's summer clothes. Choosing a flannel suit in May is one of the moments of one's life—only equalled by certain other great moments at the hosier's and hatter's. "Ne'er cast a clout till May be out" says a particularly idiotic saw, but as you have already disregarded it by casting your fur coat, you may as well go through with the business now. Socks; I ask you to think of summer socks. Have you ordered your half-hose yet? No. Then how can you go away for your holiday?

Again, taxicabs pull down their shutters in May, and you are able to see and be seen as you drive through London. Never forget when you drive in a taxi that you own the car absolutely as long as the clock is ticking; that you are a motorist, a fit member for the Royal Automobile Club; that the driver is your chauffeur to obey your orders; and, best of all, that, May being here, you can put your feet upon the seat opposite in the sight of everybody. Will you miss the glory? In June and July it will have lost something. Pay your five shillings in May and expand, live; pay your five pounds if you like and drive all down the Cromwell Road. Don't bury yourself in Devonshire.

The long light evenings of June in London! The dances, the dinners in the warm nights of June! The window-boxes in the squares, the pretty people in the parks; are we going to leave them? There is so much going on. We may not be in it, but we must be in London to feel that we are helping. They also serve who only stand and stare. Besides—I put it to you—strawberries are ripe in June. You will never get enough in Cumberland or wherever you are. Not good ones; not the shilling-a-seed kind.

Is it wise to go away in July? What about the Varsity match and Gentlemen v. Players? You must be at Lord's for those. Yes; July is the month for Lord's. Drive there, I beg you, in a hansom, if indeed there is still one left. A taxi by all means in May or when you are in a hurry, but a day at Lord's must be taken deliberately. Drive there at your leisure; breathe deeply. Do not be afraid of taking your seat before play begins—you can buy a Sportsman on the ground and read how Vallingwick nearly beat Upper Finchley. It is all part of the great game, and if you are to enjoy your day truly, then you must go with this feeling in the back of your mind—that you ought really to be working. That is the right condiment for a cricket match.

Yes; we must be near St. John's Wood in July, but what about August? Everybody, you say, goes away in August; but is not that rather a reason for staying? I don't bother to point out that the country will be crowded, only that London will be so pleasantly empty. In August and September you can wander about in your oldest clothes and nobody will mind. You can get a seat for any play without difficulty—indeed, without paying, if you know the way. It is a rare time for seeing the old churches of the City or for exploring the South Kensington Museum. London is not London in August and September; it is a jolly old town that you have never seen before. You can dine at the Savoy in your shirt sleeves—well, nearly. I mean, that gives you the idea. And, best of all, your friends will all be enjoying themselves in the country, and they will ask you down for week-ends. Robinson, who is having a cricket week for his schoolboy sons, and Smith, who has hired a yacht, will be glad to see you from Friday to Tuesday. If you had gone to Switzerland for the month, you couldn't have accepted their kind invitations. "How I wish," you would have said as you paid the extra centimes on their letters, "how I wish I had taken my holiday in June." On the other hand, in June— —

Well, you see how difficult it is for you. Of course, I don't really mind what you do. For myself I have almost decided to have a week in each month. The advantage of this is that I shall go away four times instead of once. There is no joy in the world to equal that of strolling after a London porter who is looking for an empty smoker in which to put your golf clubs. To do it four times, each time with the knowledge of a week's holiday ahead, is almost more than man deserves. True that by this means I shall also come back four times instead of once, but to a lover of London that is no great matter. Indeed, I like it so.

And another advantage is that I can take five weeks in this way while deluding my conscience into thinking that I am only taking four. A holiday taken in a lump is taken and over. Taken in weeks, with odd days at each end of the weeks, it always leaves a margin for error. I shall take care that the error is on the right side. And if anybody grumbles, "Why, you're always going away," I shall answer with dignity, "Confound it! I'm always coming back."

The Burlington Arcade

It is the fashion, I understand, to be late for dinner, but punctual for lunch. What the perfect gentleman does when he accepts an invitation to breakfast I do not know. Possibly he has to be early. But for lunch the guests should arrive at the very stroke of the appointed hour, even though it leads to a certain congestion on the mat.

My engagement was for one-thirty, and for a little while my reputation seemed to be in jeopardy. Two circumstances contributed to this. The first one was the ever-present difficulty in these busy days of synchronizing an arrival. A prudent man allows himself time for being pushed off the first half-dozen omnibuses and trusts to surging up with the seventh wave. I was so unlucky as to cleave my way on to the first 'bus of all, with the result that when I descended from it I was a good ten minutes early. Well, that was bad enough. But, just as I was approaching the door, I realized that my calculations had been made for a one o'clock lunch. It was now ten to one; I had forty minutes in hand.

It is very difficult to know what to do with forty minutes in the middle of Piccadilly, particularly when it is raining. Until a year ago I had had a club there, and I had actually resigned from it (how little one foresees the future!) on the plea that I never had occasion to use it. I felt that I would cheerfully have paid the subscription for the rest of my life in order to have had the loan of its roof at that moment. My new club—like the National Gallery and the British Museum, those refuges for the wet Londoner—was too far away. The Academy had not yet opened.

And then a sudden inspiration drew me into the Burlington Arcade. They say that the churches of London are ill-attended nowadays, but at least St. James, Piccadilly, can have no cause for complaint, for I suppose that the merchants of the Arcade, and all those dependent on them, repair thither twice weekly to pray for wet weather. The Burlington Arcade is indeed a beautiful place on a wet day. One can move leisurely from window to window, passing from silk pyjamas to bead necklaces and from bead necklaces back to silk pyjamas again; one can look for a break in the weather from either the north or the south; and at the south end there is a clock conveniently placed for those who have a watch waiting its turn at the repairer's and a luncheon engagement in forty minutes.

For a long time I hesitated between a bead necklace and a pair of pyjamas. A few coloured stones on a chain were introduced to the umbrella-less onlooker as "The Latest Fashion," followed by the announcement, superfluous in the circumstances, that it was "Very Stylish." It came as a shock to read further that one could be in the fashion for so little a sum as six shillings. There were other necklaces at the same price but of entirely different design, which were equally "Stylish," and of a fashion no less up to date. In this the merchant seemed to me to have made a mistake; for the whole glory of wearing "The Latest Fashion" is the realization that the other woman has just missed it by a bead or two. A fashion must be exclusive. St. James, Piccadilly, is all very well, but one has also to consider how to draw the umbrella-less within after one has got their noses to the shop window.

I passed on to the pyjamas, which seemed to be mostly in regimental colours. This war came upon us too suddenly, so that most of us rushed into the army without a proper consideration of essentials. I doubt if anyone who enlisted in the early days stopped to ask himself whether the regimental colours would suit him. It will be different in the next war. If anybody joins the infantry at all (which is doubtful), he will at least join a regiment whose pyjamas may be worn with self-respect in the happy peace days.

There are objections to turning up to lunch (however warmly invited) with a pair of pyjamas under the arm. It looks as though you might stay too long. I moved on to another row of bead necklaces. They offered themselves for two shillings, and all that the owner could find to say for them was that they were "Quite New." If he meant that nobody had ever worn such a necklace before, he was probably right, but I feel that he could have done better for them than this, and that, "As supplied to the Queen of Denmark," or something of the sort, would have justified an increase to two and threepence.

By this time nearly everybody was lunching except myself, and my clock said one twenty-five. If I were to arrive with that exact punctuality upon which I so credit myself, I must buy my bead necklace upon some other day. I said good-bye to the Burlington Arcade, and stepped out of it with the air of a man who has done a successful morning's shopping. A clock in the hall was striking one-thirty as I entered. Then I remembered. It was Tuesday's lunch which was to be at one-thirty. To-day's was at one o'clock... However, I had discovered the Burlington Arcade.

State Lotteries

The popular argument against the State Lottery is an assertion that it will encourage the gambling spirit. The popular argument in favour of the State Lottery is an assertion that it is hypocritical to say that it will encourage the gambling spirit, because the gambling spirit is already amongst us. Having listened to a good deal of this sort of argument on both sides, I thought it would be well to look up the word "gamble" in my dictionary. I found it next to "gamboge," and I can now tell you all about it.

To gamble, says my dictionary, is "to play for money in games of skill or chance," and it adds the information that the word is derived from the Anglo-Saxon gamen, which means "a game". Now, to me this definition is particularly interesting, because it justifies all that I have been thinking about the gambling spirit in connexion with Premium Bonds. I am against Premium Bonds, but not for the popular reason. I am against them because (as it seems to me) there is so very little of the gamble about them. And now that I have looked up "gamble" in the dictionary, I see that I was right. The "chance" element in a state lottery is obvious enough, but the "game" element is entirely absent. It is nothing so harmless and so human as the gambling spirit which Premium Bonds would encourage.

We play for money in games of skill or chance—bridge, for instance. But it isn't only of the money we are thinking. We get pleasure out of the game. Probably we prefer it to a game of greater chance, such as vingt-et-un. But even at vingt-et-un or baccarat there is something more than chance which is taking a hand in the game; not skill, perhaps, but at least personality. If you are only throwing dice, you are engaged in a personal struggle with another man, and you are directing the struggle to this extent, that you can call the value of the stakes, and decide whether to go on or to stop. And is there any man who, having made a fortune at Monte Carlo, will admit that he owes it entirely to chance? Will he not rather attribute it to his wonderful system, or if not to that, at any rate to his wonderful nerve, his perseverance, or his recklessness?

The "game" element, then, comes into all these forms of gambling, and still more strongly does it pervade that most common form of gambling, betting on horses. I do not suggest that the street-corner boy who puts a shilling both ways on Bronchitis knows anything whatever about horses, but at least he thinks he does; and if he wins five shillings on that happy afternoon when Bronchitis proves himself to be the 2.30 winner, his pleasure will not be solely in the money. The thought that he is such a skilful follower of form, that he has something of the national eye for a horse, will give him as much pleasure as can be extracted from the five shillings itself.

This, then, is the gambling spirit. It has its dangers, certainly, hut it is not entirely an evil spirit. It is possible that the State should not encourage it, but it is not called upon to exorcise it with bell, and book, and candle. I am not sure that I should favour a State gamble, but my arguments against it would be much the same as my arguments against State cricket or the solemn official endowment and recognition of any other jolly game. However, I need not trouble you with those arguments now, for nothing so harmless as a State gamble has ever been suggested. Instead, we have from time to time a State lottery offered to us, and that is a very different proposition.

For in a State lottery—with daily prizes of £50,000—the game (or gambling) element does not exist. Buy your £100 bond, as a thousand placards will urge you to do, and you simply take part in a cold-blooded attempt to acquire money without working for it. You can take no personal interest whatever in the manner of acquiring it. Somebody turns a handle, and perhaps your number comes out. More probably it doesn't. If it doesn't, you can call yourself a fool for having thrown away your savings; if it does— well, you have got the money. May you be happy with it! But you have considerably less on which to congratulate yourself than had the street-corner boy who backed Bronchitis. He had an eye for a horse. Probably you hadn't even an eye for a row of figures.

Moreover, the State would be giving its official approval to the unearned fortune. In these days, when the worker is asking for a week of so many less hours and so many more shillings, the State would answer: "I can show you a better way than that. What do you say to no work at all, and £20 a week for it?" At a time when the one cry is "Production!" the State adds (behind its hand), "Buy a Premium Bond, and let the other man produce for you." After all these years in which we have been slowly progressing towards the idea of a more equitable distribution of wealth, the Government would show us the really equitable way; it would collect the savings of the many, and re-distribute them among the few. Instead of a million ten-pound citizens, we should have a thousand ten-thousand-pounders and 999,000 with nothing. That would be the official way of making the country happy and contented. But, in fact, our social and political controversies are not kept alive by such arguments as these, nor by the answers which can legitimately be made to such arguments. The case of the average man in favour of State lotteries is, quite simply, that he does not like Dr. Clifford. The case of the average man against State lotteries is equally simple; he cannot bear to be on the same side as Mr. Bottomley.

The Record Lie

I have just seen it quoted again. Yes, it appears solemnly in print, even now, at the end of the greatest war in history. Si vis pacem, para bellum. And the writer goes on to say that the League of Nations is all very well, but unfortunately we are "not angels." Dear, dear!

Being separated for the moment from my book of quotations, I cannot say who was the Roman thinker who first gave this brilliant paradox to the world, but I imagine him a fat, easy-going gentleman, who occasionally threw off good things after dinner. He never thought very much of Si vis pacem, para bellum; it was not one of his best; but it seemed to please some of his political friends, one of whom asked if he might use it in his next speech in the Senate. Our fat gentleman said: "Certainly, if you like," and added, with unusual frankness: "I don't quite know what it means." But the other did not think that that would matter very much. So he quoted it, and it had a considerable vogue... and by and by they returned to the place from which they had come, leaving behind them the record of the ages, the lie which has caused more suffering than anything the Devil could have invented for himself. Two thousand years from now people will still be quoting it, and killing each other on the strength of it. Or perhaps I am wrong. Perhaps two thousand years from now, if the English language is sufficiently dead by then, the world will have some casual paradox of Bernard Shaw's or Oscar Wilde's on its lips, passing it reverently from mouth to mouth as if it were Holy Writ, and dropping bombs on Mars to show that they know what it means. For a quotation is a handy thing to have about, saving one the trouble of thinking for oneself, always a laborious business.

Si vis pacem, para bellum. Yes, it sounds well. It has a conclusive ring about it, particularly if the speaker stops there for a moment and drinks a glass of water. "If you want peace, prepare for war," is not quite so convincing; that might have been his own idea, evolved while running after a motor-bus in the morning; we should not be so ready to accept it as Gospel. But Si vis pacem — —! It is almost blasphemous to doubt it.

Suppose for a moment that it is true. Well, but this certainly is true: Si vis bellum, para bellum. So it follows that preparation for war means nothing; it does not necessarily mean that you want war, it does not necessarily mean that you want peace; it is an action which is as likely to have been inspired by an evil motive as by a good motive. When a gentleman with a van calls for your furniture you have means of ascertaining whether he is the furniture-remover whom you ordered or the burglar whom you didn't order, but there is no way of discovering which of two Latin tags is inspiring a nation's armaments. Si vis pacem, para bellum — it is a delightful excuse. Germany was using it up to the last moment.

However, I can produce a third tag in the same language, which is worth consideration. Si vis amare bellum, para bellum — said by Quintus Balbus the Younger five minutes before he was called a pro-Carthaginian. There seems to be something in it. I have been told by women that it is great fun putting on a new frock, but I understand that they like going out in it afterwards. After years in the schools a painter does want to show the public what he has learnt. Soldiers who have given their lives to preparing for war may be different; they may be quite content to play about at manoeuvres and answer examination papers. I learnt my golf (such as it is) by driving into a net. Perhaps, if I had had the soldier's temperament, I should still be driving into a net quite happily. On the other hand, soldiers may be just like other people, and having prepared for a thing may want to do it.

No; it is a pity, but Universal Peace will hardly come as the result of universal preparedness for war, as these dear people seem to hope. It will only come as the result of a universal feeling that war is the most babyish and laughably idiotic thing that this poor world has evolved. Our writer says sadly that there is no hope of doing without armies—we are not angels. It is not a question of "not being angels," it is a question of not being childish lunatics. Possibly there is no hope of this either, but I think we might make an effort.

For opinions do spread, if one holds them firmly oneself and is not afraid of confessing them. A si-vis-pacem gentleman said to me once, with a sneer: "How are you going to do it? Speeches and pamphlets?" Well, that was how Christianity got about, even though Paul's letters did not appear in a daily paper with a circulation of a million and a telegraphic service to every part of the world.

But perhaps Christianity is an unfortunate example to give in an argument about war; one begins to ask oneself if Christianity has spread as much as one thought. There are dear people, of course, to whom it has been revealed in the night that God is really much more interested in nations than in persons; it is not your soul or my soul that He is concerned about, but the British Empire's. Germany He dislikes (although the Germans were under a silly misapprehension about this once), and though the Japanese do not worship Him, yet they are such active little fellows, not to say Allies of England, that they too are under His special protection. And when He deprecated lying and stealing and murder and bearing false witness, and all those things, He meant that if they were done in a really wholesale way—by nations, not by individuals—then it did not matter; for He can forgive a nation anything, having so much more interest in it. All of which may be true, but it is not Christianity.

However, as our writer says, "we are not angels," and apparently he thinks that it would be rather wicked of us to try to be. Perhaps he is right.

Wedding Bells

Champagne is often pleasant at lunch, it is always delightful at dinner, and it is an absolute necessity, if one is to talk freely about oneself afterwards, at a dance supper. But champagne for tea is horrible. Perhaps this is why a wedding always finds me melancholy next morning. "She has married the wrong man," I say to myself. "I wonder if it is too late to tell her."

The trouble of answering the invitation and of thinking of something to give more original than a toast rack should, one feels, have its compensations. From each wedding that I attend I expect an afternoon's enjoyment in return for my egg stand. For one thing I have my best clothes on. Few people have seen me in them (and these few won't believe it), so that from the very beginning the day has a certain freshness. It is not an ordinary day. It starts with this advantage, that in my best clothes I am not difficult to please. The world smiles upon me.

Once I am in church, however, my calm begins to leave me. As time wears on, and the organist invents more and more tunes, I tremble lest the bride has forgotten the day. The choir is waiting for her; the bridegroom is waiting for her. I—I also—wait. What if she has changed her mind at the last minute? But no. The organist has sailed into his set piece; the choir advances; follows the bride looking so lonely that I long to comfort her and remind her of my egg stand; and, last of all, the pretty bridesmaids. The clergyman begins his drone.

You would think that, reassured by the presence of the bride, I could be happy now. But there is still much to bother me. The bridegroom is showing signs of having forgotten his part, the bride can't get her glove off, one of the bridesmaids is treading on my hat. Worse than all this, there is a painful want of unanimity among the congregation as to when we stand up and when we sit down. Sometimes I am alone and sitting when everybody else is standing, and that is easy to bear; but sometimes I find myself standing when everybody else is sitting, and that is very hard.

They have gone to the vestry. The choir sings an anthem to while away the kissing-time, and, right or wrong, I am sitting down, comforting my poor hat. There was a time when I, too, used to go into the vestry; when I was something of an authority on weddings, and would attend weekly in some minor official capacity. Any odd jobs that were going seemed to devolve on me. If somebody was wanted suddenly to sign the register, or kiss the bride's mother, or wind up the going-away car, it used to be taken for granted that I was the man to do it. I wore a white flower in my button-hole to show that I was available. I served, I may say, in an entirely honorary capacity, except in so far as I was expected to give the happy pair a slightly larger present than the others. One day I happened to suggest to an intending groom that he had other friends more ornamental, and therefore more suitable for this sort of work, than I; to which he replied that they were all married, and that etiquette demanded a bachelor for the business. Of course, as soon as I heard this I got married too.

Here they come. "Doesn't she look sweet?" We hurry after them and rush for the carriages. I am only a friend of the bridegroom's; perhaps I had better walk.

It must be very easy to be a guest at a wedding reception, where each of the two clans takes it for granted that all the extraordinary strangers belong to the other clan. Indeed, nobody with one good suit, and a stomach for champagne and sandwiches, need starve in London. He or she can wander safely in wherever a red carpet beckons. I suppose I must put in an appearance at this reception, but if I happen to pass another piece of carpet on the way to the house, and the people going in seem more attractive than our lot, I shall be tempted to join them.

This is, perhaps, the worst part of the ceremony, this three hundred yards or so from the hymn-sheets to the champagne. All London is now gazing at my old top-hat. When the war went on and on and on, and it seemed as though it were going on for ever, I looked back on peace much as those old retired warriors at the end of last century looked back on their happy Crimean days; and in the same spirit as that in which they hung their swords over the baronial fireplace, I decided to suspend my old top-hat above the mantelpiece in the drawing-room. In the years to come I would take my grandchildren on my knee and tell them stories of the old days when grandfather was a civilian, of desperate charges by churchwardens and organists, and warm receptions; and sometimes I would hold the old top-hat reverently in my hands, and a sudden gleam would come into my eyes, so that those watching me would say to each other, "He is thinking of that tea-fight at Rutland Gate in 1912." So I pictured the future for my top-hat, never dreaming that in 1920 it would take the air again.

For I went into the war in order to make the world safe for democracy, which I understood to mean (and was distinctly informed so by the press) a world safe for those of us who prefer soft hats with a dent in the middle. "The war," said the press, "has killed the top-hat." Apparently it failed to do this, as it failed to do so many of the things which we hoped from it. So the old veteran of 1912 dares the sunlight again. We are arrived, and I am greeted warmly by the bride's parents. I look at the mother closely so that I shall know her again when I come to say good-bye, and give her a smile which tells her that I was determined to come down to this wedding although I had a good deal of work to do. I linger with the idea of pursuing this point, for I want them to know that they nearly missed me, but I am pushed on by the crowd behind me. The bride and bridegroom salute me cordially but show no desire for intimate gossip. A horrible feeling goes through me that my absence would not have been commented upon by them at any inordinate length. It would not have spoilt the honeymoon, for instance.

I move on and look at the presents. The presents are numerous and costly. Having discovered my own I stand a little way back and listen to the opinions of my neighbours upon it. On the whole the reception is favourable. The detective, I am horrified to discover, is on the other side of the room, apparently callous as to the fate of my egg stand. I cannot help feeling that if he knew his business he would be standing where I am standing now; or else there should be two detectives. It is a question now whether it is safe for me to leave my post and search for food... Now he is coming round; I can trust it to him.

On my way to the refreshments I have met an old friend. I like to meet my friends at weddings, but I wish I had not met this one. She has sowed the seeds of disquiet in my mind by telling me that it is not etiquette to begin to eat until the bride has cut the cake. I answer, "Then why doesn't somebody tell the bride to cut the cake?" but the bride, it seems, is busy. I wish now that I had not met my friend. Who but a woman would know the etiquette of these things, and who but a woman would bother about it?

The bride is cutting the cake. The bridegroom has lent her his sword, or his fountain-pen, whatever is the emblem of his trade—he is a stockbroker—and as she cuts, we buzz round her, hoping for one of the marzipan pieces. I wish to leave now, before I am sorry, but my friend tells me that it is not etiquette to leave until the bride and bridegroom have gone. Besides, I must drink the bride's health. I drink her health; hers, not mine.

Time rolls on. I was wrong to have had champagne. It doesn't suit me at tea. However, for the moment life is bright enough. I have looked at the presents and my own is still there. And I have been given a bagful of confetti. The weary weeks one lives through without a handful of anything to throw at anybody. How good to be young again. I take up a strong position in the hall.

They come... Got him—got him! Now a long shot—got him! I feel slightly better, and begin the search for my hostess....

I have shaken hands with all the bride's aunts and all the bridegroom's aunts, and in fact all the aunts of everybody here.

Each one seems to me more like my hostess than the last. "Good-bye!" Fool—of course—there she is. "Good-Bye!"

My hat and I take the air again. A pleasant afternoon; and yet to-morrow morning I shall see things more clearly, and I shall know that the bridegroom has married the wrong girl. But it will be too late then to save him.

Public Opinion

At the beginning of the last strike the papers announced that Public Opinion was firmly opposed to dictation by a minority. Towards the end of the strike the papers said that Public Opinion was strongly in favour of a settlement which would leave neither side with a sense of defeat. I do not complain of either of these statements, but I have been wondering, as I have often wondered before, how a leader-writer discovers what the Public Opinion is.

When one reads about Public Opinion in the press (and one reads a good deal about it one way and another), it is a little difficult to realize, particularly if the printer has used capital letters, that this much-advertised Public Opinion is simply You and Me and the Others. Now, since it is impossible for any man to get at the opinions of all of us, it is necessary that he should content himself with a sample half-dozen or so. But from where does he get his sample? Possibly from his own club, limited perhaps to men of his own political opinions; almost certainly from his own class. Public Opinion in this case is simply what he thinks. Even if he takes the opinion of strangers—the waiter who serves him at lunch, the tobacconist, the policeman at the corner—the opinion may be one specially prepared for his personal consumption, one inspired by tact, boredom, or even a sense of humour. If, for instance, the process were to be reversed, and my tobacconist were to ask me what I thought of the strike, I should grunt and go out of his shop; but he would be wrong to attribute "a dour grimness" to the nation in consequence.

Nor is the investigator likely to be more correct if he judges Public Opinion from the evidence of his eyes rather than his ears. Thus one reporter noticed on the faces of his companions in the omnibus "a look of stern determination to see this thing through." If they were all really looking like that, it must have been an impressive sight. But it is at least possible that this distinctive look was one of stern determination to get a more comfortable seat on the 'bus which took them home again.

It must be very easy (and would certainly be extremely interesting) to go about forming Public Opinion, I should like to initiate an L.F.P.O., or League for Forming Public Opinion, and not only for forming it, but for putting it, when formed, into direct action. Such a League, even if limited to two hundred members, could by its concerted action exercise a very remarkable effect. Suppose we decided to attack profiteering. We should choose our shop—a hosier's, let us say. Beginning on Monday morning, a member of the League would go in and ask to be shown some ties. Having spent some time in looking through the stock and selecting a couple, he would ask the price. "Oh, but that's ridiculous," he would say. "I couldn't think of paying that. If I can't get them cheaper somewhere else, I'll do without them altogether." The shopman shrugs his shoulders and puts his ties back again. Perhaps he tells himself contemptuously that he doesn't cater for that sort of customer. The customer goes out, and half an hour later the second member of the League arrives. This one asks for collars. He is equally indignant at the price, and is equally determined not to wear a collar at all rather than submit to such extortion. Half an hour later the third member comes in. He wants socks.... The fourth member wants ties again... The fifth wants gloves....

Now this is going on, not only all through the day, but all through the week, and for another week after that. Can you not imagine that, after a fortnight of it, the haberdasher begins to feel that "Public Opinion is strongly aroused against profiteering in the hosiery trade"? Is it not possible that the loss of two hundred customers in a fortnight would make him wonder whether a lower price might not bring him in a greater profit? I think it is possible. I do not think he could withstand a Public Opinion so well organized and so relentlessly concentrated.

But such a League would have enormous power in many ways. If you were to write to the editor of a paper complaining that So-and-

So's contributions (mine, if you like) were beneath contempt, the editor would not be seriously concerned about it. Possibly he had a letter the day before saying that So-and-So was beyond all other writers delightful. But if twenty members of the League wrote every week for ten weeks in succession, from two hundred different addresses, saying that So-and-So's articles were beneath contempt, the editor would be more than human if he did not tell himself that So-and-So had fallen off a little and was obviously losing his hold on the popular imagination. In a little while he would decide that it would be wiser to make a change....

Of course, the League would not attack a writer or any other public man from sheer wilfulness, but it would probably have no difficulty in bringing down over-praised mediocrity to its proper level or in giving a helping hand to unrecognized talent. But unless its president were a man of unerring judgment and remarkable restraint, its sense of power would probably be too much for it, and it would lose its head altogether. Looking round for a suitable president, I can think of nobody but myself. And I am too busy just now.

The Honour of Your Country

We were resting after the first battle of the Somme. Naturally all the talk in the Mess was of after-the-war. Ours was the H.Q. Mess, and I was the only subaltern; the youngest of us was well over thirty. With a gravity befitting our years and (except for myself) our rank, we discussed not only restaurants and revues, but also Reconstruction.

The Colonel's idea of Reconstruction included a large army of conscripts. He did not call them conscripts. The fact that he had chosen to be a soldier himself, out of all the professions open to him, made it difficult for him to understand why a million others should not do the same without compulsion. At any rate, we must have the men. The one thing the war had taught us was that we must have a real Continental army.

I asked why. "Theirs not to reason why" on parade, but in the H.Q. Mess on active service the Colonel is a fellow human being. So I asked him why we wanted a large army after the war.

For the moment he was at a loss. Of course, he might have said "Germany," had it not been decided already that there would be no Germany after the war. He did not like to say "France," seeing that we were even then enjoying the hospitality of the most delightful French villages. So, after a little hesitation, he said "Spain."

At least he put it like this:—

"Of course, we must have an army, a large army."

"But why?" I said again.

"How else can you—can you defend the honour of your country?"

"The Navy."

"The Navy! Pooh! The Navy isn't a weapon of attack; it's a weapon of defence."

"But you said 'defend'."

"Attack," put in the Major oracularly, "is the best defence."

"Exactly."

I hinted at the possibilities of blockade. The Colonel was scornful. "Sitting down under an insult for months and months," he called it, until you starved the enemy into surrender. He wanted something much more picturesque, more immediately effective than that. (Something, presumably, more like the Somme.)

"But give me an example," I said, "of what you mean by 'insults' and 'honour'."

Whereupon he gave me this extraordinary example of the need for a large army.

"Well, supposing," he said, "that fifty English women in Madrid were suddenly murdered, what would you do?"

I thought for a moment, and then said that I should probably decide not to take my wife to Madrid until things had settled down a bit.

"I'm supposing that you're Prime Minister," said the Colonel, a little annoyed. "What is England going to do?"

"Ah!... Well, one might do nothing. After all, what is one to do? One can't restore them to life."

The Colonel, the Major, even the Adjutant, expressed his contempt for such a cowardly policy. So I tried again.

"Well," I said, "I might decide to murder fifty Spanish women in London, just to even things up."

The Adjutant laughed. But the Colonel was taking it too seriously for that.

"Do you mean it?" he asked.

"Well, what would you do, sir?"

"Land an army in Spain," he said promptly, "and show them what it meant to treat English women like that."

"I see. They would resist of course?"

"No doubt."

"Yes. But equally without doubt we should win in the end?"

"Certainly."

"And so re-establish England's honour."

"Quite so."

"I see. Well, sir, I really think my way is the better. To avenge the fifty murdered English women, you are going to kill (say) 100,000 Spaniards who have had no connexion with the murders, and 50,000 Englishmen who are even less concerned. Indirectly also you will cause the death of hundreds of guiltless Spanish women and children, besides destroying the happiness of thousands of English wives and mothers. Surely my way—of murdering only fifty innocents—is just as effective and much more humane."

"That's nonsense," said the Colonel shortly.

"And the other is war."

We were silent for a little, and then the Colonel poured himself out a whisky.

"All the same," he said, as he went back to his seat, "you haven't answered my question."

"What was that, sir?"

"What you would do in the case I mentioned. Seriously."

"Oh! Well, I stick to my first answer. I would do nothing—except, of course, ask for an explanation and an apology. If you can apologize for that sort of thing."

"And if they were refused?"

"Have no more official relations with Spain."

"That's all you would do?"

"Yes."

"And you think that that is consistent with the honour of a great nation like England?"

"Perfectly."

"Oh! Well, I don't."

An indignant silence followed.

"May I ask you a question now, sir?" I said at last.

"Well?"

"Suppose this time England begins. Suppose we murder all the Spanish women in London first. What are you going to do—as Spanish Premier?"

"Er—I don't quite——"

"Are you going to order the Spanish Fleet to sail for the mouth of the Thames, and hurl itself upon the British fleet?"

"Of course not, She has no fleet."

"Then do you agree with the—er Spanish Colonel, who goes about saying that Spain's honour will never be safe until she has a fleet as big as England's?"

"That's ridiculous. They couldn't possibly."

"Then what could Spain do in the circumstances?"

"Well, she—er—she could—er—protest."

"And would that be consistent with the honour of a small nation like Spain?"

"In the circumstances," said the Colonel unwillingly, "er—yes."

"So that what it comes to is this. Honour only demands that you should attack the other man if you are much bigger than he is. When a man insults my wife, I look him carefully over; if he is a stone heavier than I, then I satisfy my honour by a mild protest. But if he only has one leg, and is three stone lighter, honour demands that I should jump on him."

"We're talking of nations," said the Colonel gruffly, "not of men, It's a question of prestige."

"Which would be increased by a victory over Spain?"

The Major began to get nervous. After all, I was only a subaltern. He tried to cool the atmosphere a little.

"I don't know why poor old Spain should be dragged into it like this," he said, with a laugh. "I had a very jolly time in Madrid years ago."

"O, I only gave Spain as an example," said the Colonel casually.

"It might just as well have been Switzerland?" I suggested.

There was silence for a little.

"Talking of Switzerland——" I said, as I knocked out my pipe.

"Oh, go on," said the Colonel, with a good-humoured shrug. "I've brought this on myself."

"Well, sir, what I was wondering was—What would happen to the honour of England if fifty English women were murdered at Interlaken?"

83

The Colonel was silent.

"However large an army we had——" I went on.

The Colonel struck a match.

"It's a funny thing, honour," I said. "And prestige."

The Colonel pulled at his pipe.

"Just fancy," I murmured, "the Swiss can do what they like to British subjects in Switzerland, and we can't get at them. Yet England's honour does not suffer, the world is no worse a place to live in, and one can spend quite a safe holiday at Interlaken."

"I remember being there in '94," began the Major hastily....

A Village Celebration

Although our village is a very small one, we had fifteen men serving in the Forces before the war was over. Fortunately, as the Vicar well said, "we were wonderfully blessed in that none of us was called upon to make the great sacrifice." Indeed, with the exception of Charlie Rudd, of the Army Service Corps, who was called upon to be kicked by a horse, the village did not even suffer any casualties. Our rejoicings at the conclusion of Peace were whole-hearted.

Naturally, when we met to discuss the best way in which to give expression to our joy, our first thoughts were with our returned heroes. Miss Travers, who plays the organ with considerable expression on Sundays, suggested that a drinking fountain erected on the village green would be a pleasing memorial of their valour, if suitably inscribed. For instance, it might say, "In gratitude to our brave defenders who leaped to answer their country's call," followed by their names. Embury, the cobbler, who is always a wet blanket on these occasions, asked if "leaping" was the exact word for a young fellow who got into khaki in 1918, and then only in answer to his country's police. The meeting was more lively after this, and Mr. Bates, of Hill Farm, had to be personally assured by the Vicar that for his part he quite understood how it was that young Robert Bates had been unable to leave the farm before, and he was sure that our good friend Embury meant nothing personal by his, if he might say so, perhaps somewhat untimely observation. He would suggest himself that some such phrase as "who gallantly answered" would be more in keeping with Miss Travers' beautiful idea. He would venture to put it to the meeting that the inscription should be amended in this sense.

Mr. Clayton, the grocer and draper, interrupted to say that they were getting on too fast. Supposing they agreed upon a drinking fountain, who was going to do it? Was it going to be done in the village, or were they going to get sculptors and architects and such-like people from London? And if so The Vicar caught the eye of Miss Travers, and signalled to her to proceed; whereupon she explained that, as she had already told the Vicar in private, her nephew was studying art in London, and she was sure he would be only too glad to get Augustus James or one of those Academy artists to think of something really beautiful.

At this moment Embury said that he would like to ask two questions. First question—In what order were the names of our gallant defenders to be inscribed? The Vicar said that, speaking entirely without preparation and on the spur of the moment, he would imagine that an alphabetical order would be the most satisfactory. There was a general "Hear, hear," led by the Squire, who thus made his first contribution to the debate. "That's what I thought," said Embury. "Well, then, second question—What's coming out of the fountain?" The Vicar, a little surprised, said that presumably, my dear Embury, the fountain would give forth water. "Ah!" said Embury with great significance, and sat down.

Our village is a little slow at getting on to things; "leaping" is not the exact word for our movements at any time, either of brain or body. It is not surprising, therefore, that even Bates failed to realize for a moment that his son's name was to have precedence on a water-fountain. But when once he realized it, he refused to be pacified by the cobbler's explanation that he had only said "Ah!" Let those who had anything to say, he observed, speak out openly, and then we should know where we were. Embury's answer, that one could generally guess where some people were, and not be far wrong, was drowned in the ecclesiastical applause which greeted the rising of the Squire.

The Squire said that he—er—hadn't—er—intended—er—to say anything. But he thought—er—if he might—er—intervene—to—er—say something on the matter of—er—a matter which—er—well, they all knew what it was—in short—er—money. Because until they knew how they—er—stood, it was obvious that—it was obvious—quite obvious—well it was a question of how they stood. Whereupon he sat down.

The Vicar said that as had often happened before, the sound common-sense of Sir John had saved them from undue rashness and precipitancy. They were getting on a little too fast. Their valued friend Miss Travers had made what he was not ashamed to call a suggestion both rare and beautiful, but alas! in these prosaic modern days the sordid question of pounds, shillings and pence could not be wholly disregarded. How much money would they have?

Everybody looked at Sir John. There was an awkward silence, in which the Squire joined....

Amid pushings and whisperings from his corner of the room, Charlie Rudd said that he would just like to say a few words for the boys, if all were willing. The Vicar said that certainly, certainly he might, my dear Rudd. So Charlie said that he would just like to say that with all respect to Miss Travers, who was a real lady, and many was the packet of fags he'd had from her out there, and all the other boys could say the same, and if some of them joined up sooner than others, well perhaps they did, but they all tried to do their bit, just like those who stayed at home, and they'd thrashed Jerry, and glad of it, fountains or no fountains, and pleased to be back again and see them all, just the same as ever, Mr. Bates and Mr. Embury and all of them, which was all he wanted to say, and the other boys would say the same, hoping no offence was meant, and that was all he wanted to say.

When the applause had died down, Mr. Clayton said that, in his opinion, as he had said before, they were getting on too fast. Did they want a fountain, that was the question. Who wanted it? The Vicar replied that it would be a beautiful memento for their children of the stirring times through which their country had passed. Embury asked if Mr. Bates' child wanted a memento of— — "This is a general question, my dear Embury," said the Vicar.

There rose slowly to his feet the landlord of the Dog and Duck. Celebrations, he said. We were celebrating this here peace. Now, as man to man, what did celebrations mean? He asked any of them. What did it mean? Celebrations meant celebrating, and celebrating meant sitting down hearty-like, sitting down like Englishmen and—and celebrating. First, find how much money they'd got, same as Sir John said; that was right and proper. Then if so be as they wanted to leave the rest to him, well he'd be proud to do his best for them. They knew him. Do fair by him and he'd do fair by them. Soon as he knew how much money they'd got, and how many were going to sit down, then he could get to work. That was all he'd got to say about celebrations.

The enthusiasm was tremendous. Rut the Vicar looked anxious, and whispered to the Squire. The Squire shrugged his shoulders and murmured something, and the Vicar rose. They would be all glad to hear, he said, glad but not surprised, that with his customary generosity the Squire had decided to throw open his own beautiful gardens and pleasure-grounds to them on Peace Day and to take upon his own shoulders the burden of entertaining them. He would suggest that they now give Sir John three hearty cheers. This was done, and the proceedings closed.

A Train of Thought

On the same day I saw two unsettling announcements in the papers. The first said simply, underneath a suitable photograph, that the ski-ing season was now in full swing in Switzerland; the second explained elaborately why it cost more to go from London to the Riviera and back than from the Riviera to London and back. Both announcements unsettled me considerably. They would upset anybody for whom the umbrella season in London was just opening, and who was wondering what was the cost of a return ticket to Manchester.

At first I amused myself with trying to decide whether I should prefer it to be the Riviera or Switzerland this Christmas. Switzerland won; not because it is more invigorating, but because I had just discovered a woollen helmet and a pair of ski-ing boots, relics of an earlier visit. I am thus equipped for Switzerland already, whereas for the Riviera I should want several new suits. One of the chief beauties of Switzerland (other than the mountains) is that it is so uncritical of the visitor's wardrobe. So long as he has a black coat for the evenings, it demands nothing more. In the day-time he may fall about in whatever he pleases. Indeed, it is almost an economy to go there now and work off some of one's moth-collecting khaki on it. The socks which are impossible with our civilian clothes could renew their youth as the middle pair of three, inside a pair of ski-ing boots.

Yet to whichever I went this year, Switzerland or the Riviera, I think it would be money wasted. I am one of those obvious people who detest an uncomfortable railway journey, and the journey this year will certainly be uncomfortable. But I am something more than this; I am one of those uncommon people who enjoy a comfortable railway journey. I mean that I enjoy it as an entertainment in itself, not only as a relief from the hair-shirts of previous journeys. I would much sooner go by wagonlit from Calais to Monte Carlo in twenty hours, than by magic carpet in twenty seconds. I am even looking forward to my journey to Manchester, supposing that there is no great rush for the place on my chosen day. The scenery as one approaches Manchester may not be beautiful, but I shall be quite happy in my corner facing the engine.

Nowhere can I think so happily as in a train. I am not inspired; nothing so uncomfortable as that. I am never seized with a sudden idea for a masterpiece, nor form a sudden plan for some new enterprise. My thoughts are just pleasantly reflective. I think of all the good deeds I have done, and (when these give out) of all the good deeds I am going to do. I look out of the window and say lazily to myself, "How jolly to live there"; and a little farther on, "How jolly not to live there." I see a cow, and I wonder what it is like to be a cow, and I wonder whether the cow wonders what it is to be like me; and perhaps, by this time, we have passed on to a sheep, and I wonder if it is more fun being a sheep. My mind wanders on in a way which would annoy Pelman a good deal, but it wanders on quite happily, and the "clankety-clank" of the train adds a very soothing accompaniment. So soothing, indeed, that at any moment I can close my eyes and pass into a pleasant state of sleep.

But this entertainment which my train provides for me is doubly entertaining if it be but the overture to greater delights. If some magic property which the train possesses—whether it be the motion or the clankety-clank—makes me happy even when I am only thinking about a cow, is it any wonder that I am happy in thinking about the delightful new life to which I am travelling? We are going to the Riviera, but I have had no time as yet in which to meditate properly upon that delightful fact. I have been too busy saving up for it, doing work in advance for it, buying cloth for it. Between London and Dover I have been worrying, perhaps, about the crossing; between Dover and Calais my worries have come to a head; but when I step into the train at Calais, then at last I can give myself up with a whole mind to the contemplation of the happy future. So long as the train does not stop, so long as nobody goes in or out of my carriage, I care not how many hours the journey takes. I have enough happy thoughts to fill them.

All this, as I said, is not at all Pelman's idea of success in life; one should be counting cows instead of thinking of them; although presumably a train journey would seem in any case a waste of time to The Man Who Succeeds. But to those of us to whom it is no more a waste of time than any other pleasant form of entertainment, the train-service to which we have had to submit lately has been doubly distressing. The bliss of travelling from London to Manchester was torn from us and we were given purgatory instead. Things are a little better now in England; if one chooses the right day one can still come sometimes upon the old happiness. But not yet on the Continent. In the happy days before the war the journey out was almost the best part of Switzerland on the Riviera. I must wait until those days come back again.

Melodrama

The most characteristic thing about a melodrama is that it always begins at 7.30. The idea, no doubt, is that one is more in the mood for this sort of entertainment after a high tea than after a late dinner. Plain living leads to plain thinking, and a solid foundation of eggs and potted meat leaves no room for appreciation of the finer shades of conduct; Right is obviously Right, and Wrong is Wrong. Or it may be also that the management wishes to allow us time for recovery afterwards from the emotions of the evening; the play ends at 10.30, so that we can build up the ravaged tissues again with a hearty supper. But whatever the reason for the early start, the result is the same. We arrive at 7.45 to find that we alone of the whole audience have been left out of the secret as to why Lord Algernon is to be pushed off the pier.

For melodrama, unlike the more fashionable comedy, gets to grips at once. It is well understood by every dramatist that a late-dining audience needs several minutes of dialogue before it recovers from its bewilderment at finding itself in a theatre at all. Even the expedient of printing the names of the characters on the programme in the order in which they appear, and of letting them address each other frankly by name as soon as they come on the stage, fails to dispel the mists. The stalls still wear that vague, flustered look, as if they had expected a concert or a prize-fight and have just remembered that the concert, of course, is to-morrow. For this reason a wise dramatist keeps back his story until the brain of the more expensive seats begins to clear, and he is careful not to waste his jokes on the first five pages of his dialogue.

But melodrama plays to cheap seats, and the purchaser of the cheap seat has come there to have his money's worth. Directly the curtain goes up he is ready to collaborate. It is perfectly safe for the Villain to come on at once and reveal his dastardly plans; the audience is alert for his confidences.

92

"Curse that young cub, Dick Vereker, what ill-fortune has sent him across my path? Already he has established himself in the affections of Lady Alicia, and if she consents to wed him my plans are foiled. Fortunately she does not know as yet that, by the will of her late Uncle Gregory, the ironmaster, two million pounds are settled upon the man who wins her hand. With two million pounds I could pay back my betting losses and prevent myself from being turned out of the Constitutional Club. And now to put the marked ace of spades in young Vereker's coat-tail pocket. Ha!"

No doubt the audience is the more ready to assimilate this because it knew it was coming. As soon as the Villain steps on to the stage he is obviously the Villain; one does not need to peer at one's programme and murmur, "Who is this, dear?" It is known beforehand that the Hero will be falsely accused, and that not until the last act will he and his true love come together again. All that we are waiting to be told is whether it is to be a marked card, a forged cheque, or a bloodstain this time; and (if, as is probable, the Heroine is forced into a marriage with the Villain) whether the Villain's first wife, whom he had deserted, will turn up during the ceremony or immediately afterwards. For the whole charm of a melodrama is that it is in essentials just like every other melodrama that has gone before. The author may indulge his own fancies to the extent of calling the Villain Jasper or Eustace, of letting the Hero be ruined on the battle-field or the Stock Exchange, but we are keeping an eye on him to see that he plays no tricks with our national drama. It is our play as well as his, and we have laid down the rules for it. Let the author stick to them.

It is strange how unconvincing the Hero is to his fellows on the stage, and how very convincing to us. That ringing voice, those gleaming eyes—how is it that none of his companions seems able to recognize Innocence when it is shining forth so obviously? "I feel that I never want to see your face again," says the Heroine, when the diamond necklace is found in his hat-box, and we feel that she has never really seen it at all yet. "Good Heavens, madam," we long to cry, "have you never been to a melodrama that you can be so deceived? Look again! Is it not the face of the Falsely Accused?" But probably she has not been to a melodrama. She moves in the best society, and the thought of a high tea at 6.30 would appal her.

But let me confess that we in the audience are carried away sometimes by that ringing voice, those gleaming eyes. He has us, this Hero, in the hollow of his hand (to borrow a phrase from the Villain). When the limelight is playing round his brow, and he stands in the centre of the stage with clenched fists, oh! then he has us. "What! Betray my aged mother for filthy gold!" he cries, looking at us scornfully as if it was our suggestion. "Never, while yet breath remains in my body!" What a cheer we give him then; a cheer which seems to imply that, having often betrayed our own mothers for half a crown or so, we are able to realize the heroic nature of his abstention on this occasion. For in the presence of the Hero we lose our sense of values. If he were to scorn an offer to sell his father for vivisectional purposes, we should applaud enthusiastically his altruism.

But it is only the Hero who wins our cheers, only the Villain who wins our hisses. The minor characters are necessary, but we are not greatly interested in them. The Villain must have a confederate to whom he can reveal his wicked thoughts when he is tired of soliloquizing; the Hero must have friends who can tell each other all those things which a modest man cannot say for himself; there must be characters of lower birth, competent to relieve the tension by sitting down on their hats or pulling chairs from beneath their acquaintances. We could not do without them, but we do not give them our hearts. Even the Heroine leaves us calm. However beautiful she be, she is not more than the Hero deserves. It is the Hero whom we have come out to see, and it is painful to reflect that in a little while he will he struggling to get on the 'bus for Walham Green, and be pushed off again just like the rest of us.

A Lost Masterpiece

The short essay on "The Improbability of the Infinite" which I was planning for you yesterday will now never be written. Last night my brain was crammed with lofty thoughts on the subject—and for that matter, on every other subject. My mind was never so fertile. Ten thousand words on any theme from Tin-tacks to Tomatoes would have been easy to me. That was last night. This morning I have only one word in my brain, and I cannot get rid of it. The word is "Teralbay."

Teralbay is not a word which one uses much in ordinary life. Rearrange the letters, however, and it becomes such a word. A friend—no, I can call him a friend no longer—a person gave me this collection of letters as I was going to bed and challenged me to make a proper word of it. He added that Lord Melbourne—this, he alleged, is a well-known historical fact—Lord Melbourne had given this word to Queen Victoria once, and it had kept her awake the whole night. After this, one could not be so disloyal as to solve it at once. For two hours or so, therefore, I merely toyed with it. Whenever I seemed to be getting warm I hurriedly thought of something else. This quixotic loyalty has been the undoing of me; my chances of a solution have slipped by, and I am beginning to fear that they will never return. While this is the case, the only word I can write about is Teralbay.

Teralbay—what does it make? There are two ways of solving a problem of this sort. The first is to waggle your eyes and see what you get. If you do this, words like "alterably" and "laboratory" emerge, which a little thought shows you to be wrong. You may then waggle your eyes again, look at it upside down or sideways, or stalk it carefully from the southwest and plunge upon it suddenly when it is not ready for you. In this way it may be surprised into giving up its secret. But if you find that it cannot be captured by strategy or assault, then there is only one way of taking

95

it. It must be starved into surrender. This will take a long time, but victory is certain.

There are eight letters in Teralbay and two of them are the same, so that there must be 181,440 ways of writing the letters out. This may not be obvious to you at once; you may have thought that it was only 181,439; but you may take my word for it that I am right. (Wait a moment while I work it out again.... Yes, that's it.) Well, now suppose that you put down a new order of letters—such as "raytable"—every six seconds, which is very easy going, and suppose that you can spare an hour a day for it; then by the 303rd day—a year hence, if you rest on Sundays—you are bound to have reached a solution.

But perhaps this is not playing the game. This, I am sure, is not what Queen Victoria did. And now I think of it, history does not tell us what she did do, beyond that she passed a sleepless night. (And that she still liked Melbourne afterwards—which is surprising.) Did she ever guess it? Or did Lord Melbourne have to tell her in the morning, and did she say, "Why, of course!" I expect so. Or did Lord Melbourne say, "I'm awfully sorry, madam, but I find I put a 'y' in too many?" But no—history could not have remained silent over such a tragedy as that. Besides, she went on liking him.

When I die "Teralbay" will be written on my heart. While I live it shall be my telegraphic address. I shall patent a breakfast food called "Teralbay"; I shall say "Teralbay!" when I miss a 2-ft. putt; the Teralbay carnation will catch your eye at the Temple show. I shall write anonymous letters over the name. "Fly at once; all is discovered—Teralbay." Yes, that would look rather well.

I wish I knew more about Lord Melbourne. What sort of words did he think of? The thing couldn't he "aeroplane" or "telephone" or "googly," because these weren't invented in his time. That gives us three words less. Nor, probably, would it be anything to eat; a Prime Minister would hardly discuss such subjects with his Sovereign. I have no doubt that after hours of immense labour you will triumphantly suggest "rateably." I suggested that myself, but it is wrong. There is no such word in the dictionary. The same objection applies to "bat-early" — it ought to mean something, but it doesn't.

So I hand the word over to you. Please do not send the solution to me, for by the time you read this I shall either have found it out or else I shall be in a nursing home. In either case it will be of no use to me. Send it to the Postmaster-General or one of the Geddeses or Mary Pickford. You will want to get it off your mind.

As for myself I shall write to my fr— —, to the person who first said "Teralbay" to me, and ask him to make something of "sabet" and "donureb." When he has worked out the corrections—which, in case he gets the wrong ones, I may tell him here are "beast" and "bounder" —I shall search the dictionary for some long word like "intellectual." I shall alter the order of the letters and throw in a couple of "g's" and a "k". And then I shall tell them to keep a spare bed for him in my nursing home.

Well, I have got "Teralbay" a little off my mind. I feel better able now to think of other things. Indeed, I might almost begin my famous essay on "The Improbability of the Infinite." It would be a pity for the country to lose such a masterpiece—she has had quite enough trouble already what with one thing and another. For my view of the Infinite is this: that although beyond the Finite, or, as one might say, the Commensurate, there may or may not be a— —

Just a moment. I think I have it now. T—R—A——No....

A Hint for Next Christmas

There has been some talk lately of the standardization of golf balls, but a more urgent reform is the standardization of Christmas presents. It is no good putting this matter off; let us take it in hand now, so that we shall be in time for next Christmas.

My crusade is on behalf of those who spend their Christmas away from home. Last year I returned (with great difficulty) from such an adventure and I am more convinced than ever that Christmas presents should conform to a certain standard of size. My own little offerings were thoughtfully chosen. A match-box, a lace handkerchief or two, a cigarette-holder, a pencil and note-book, Gems from Wilcox, and so on; such gifts not only bring pleasure (let us hope) to the recipient, but take up a negligible amount of room in one's bag, and add hardly anything to the weight of it. Of course, if your fellow-visitor says to you, "How sweet of you to give me such a darling little handkerchief—it's just what I wanted—how ever did you think of it?" you do not reply, "Well, it was a choice between that and a hundredweight of coal, and I'll give you two guesses why I chose the handkerchief." No; you smile modestly and say, "As soon as I saw it, I felt somehow that it was yours"; after which you are almost in a position to ask your host casually where he keeps the mistletoe.

But it is almost a certainty that the presents you receive will not have been chosen with such care. Probably the young son of the house has been going in for carpentry lately, and in return for your tie-pin he gives you a wardrobe of his own manufacture. You thank him heartily, you praise its figure, but all the time you are wishing that it had chosen some other occasion. Your host gives you a statuette or a large engraving; somebody else turns up with a large brass candle-stick. It is all very gratifying, but you have got to get back to London somehow, and, thankful though you are not to have received the boar-hound or parrot-in-cage which seemed at one time to be threatening, you cannot help wishing that the limits of size for a Christmas present had been decreed by some authority who was familiar with the look of your dressing-case.

Obviously, too, there should be a standard value for a certain type of Christmas present. One may give what one will to one's own family or particular friends; that is all right. But in a Christmas house-party there is a pleasant interchange of parcels, of which the string and the brown paper and the kindly thought are the really important ingredients, and the gift inside is nothing more than an excuse for these things. It is embarrassing for you if Jones has apologized for his brown paper with a hundred cigars, and you have only excused yourself with twenty-five cigarettes; perhaps still more embarrassing if it is you who have lost so heavily on the exchange. An understanding that the contents were to be worth five shillings exactly would avoid this embarassment.

And now I am reminded of the ingenuity of a friend of mine, William by name, who arrived at a large country house for Christmas without any present in his bag. He had expected neither to give nor to receive anything, but to his horror he discovered on the 24th that everybody was preparing a Christmas present for him, and that it was taken for granted that he would require a little privacy and brown paper on Christmas Eve for the purpose of addressing his own offerings to others. He had wild thoughts of telegraphing to London for something to be sent down, and spoke to other members of the house-party in order to discover what sort of presents would be suitable.

"What are you giving our host P" he asked one of them.

"Mary and I are giving him a book," said John, referring to his wife.

William then approached the youngest son of the house, and discovered that he and his next brother Dick were sharing in this, that, and the other. When he had heard this, William retired to his room and thought profoundly. He was the first down to breakfast on Christmas morning. All the places at the table were piled high with presents. He looked at John's place. The top parcel said, "To John and Mary from Charles." William took out his fountain-pen and added a couple of words to the inscription. It then read, "To John and Mary from Charles and William," and in William's opinion looked just as effective as before. He moved on to the next place. "To Angela from Father," said the top parcel. "And William," wrote William. At his hostess' place he hesitated for a moment. The first present there was for "Darling Mother, from her loving children." It did not seem that an "and William" was quite suitable. But his hostess was not to be deprived of William's kindly thought; twenty seconds later the handkerchiefs "from John and Mary and William" expressed all the nice things which he was feeling for her. He passed on to the next place....

It is, of course, impossible to thank every donor of a joint gift; one simply thanks the first person whose eye one happens to catch. Sometimes William's eye was caught, sometimes not. But he was spared all embarrassment; and I can recommend his solution of the problem with perfect confidence to those who may be in a similar predicament next Christmas.

There is a minor sort of Christmas present about which also a few words must be said; I refer to the Christmas card.

The Christmas card habit is a very pleasant one, but it, too, needs to be disciplined. I doubt if many people understand its proper function. This is partly the result of our bringing up; as children we were allowed (quite rightly) to run wild in the Christmas card shop, with one of two results. Either we still run wild, or else the reaction has set in and we avoid the Christmas card shop altogether. We convey our printed wishes for a happy Christmas to everybody or to nobody. This is a mistake. In our middle-age we should discriminate.

The child does not need to discriminate. It has two shillings in the hand and about twenty-four relations. Even in my time two shillings did not go far among twenty-four people. But though presents were out of the question, one could get twenty-four really beautiful Christmas cards for the money, and if some of them were ha'penny ones, then one could afford real snow on a threepenny one for the most important uncle, meaning by "most important," perhaps (but I have forgotten now), the one most likely to be generous in return. Of the fun of choosing those twenty-four cards I need not now speak, nor of the best method of seeing to it that somebody else paid for the necessary twenty-four stamps. But certainly one took more trouble in suiting the tastes of those who were to receive the cards than the richest and most leisured grown-up would take in selecting a diamond necklace for his wife's stocking or motor-cars for his sons-in-law. It was not only a question of snow, but also of the words in which the old, old wish was expressed. If the aunt who was known to be fond of poetry did not get something suitable from Eliza Cook, one might regard her Christmas as ruined. How could one grudge the trouble necessary to make her Christmas really happy for her? One might even explore the fourpenny box.

But in middle-age—by which I mean anything over twenty and under ninety—one knows too many people. One cannot give them a Christmas card each; there is not enough powdered glass to go round. One has to discriminate, and the way in which most of us discriminate is either to send no cards to anybody or else to send them to the first twenty or fifty or hundred of our friends (according to our income and energy) whose names come into our minds. Such cards are meaningless; but if we sent our Christmas cards to the right people, we could make the simple words upon them mean something very much more than a mere wish that the recipient's Christmas shall be "merry" (which it will be anyhow, if he likes merriness) and his New Year "bright" (which, let us hope, it will not be).

"A merry Christmas," with an old church in the background and a robin in the foreground, surrounded by a wreath of holly-leaves. It might mean so much. What I feel that it ought to mean is something like this:—

"You live at Potters Bar and I live at Petersham. Of course, if we did happen to meet at the Marble Arch one day, it would be awfully jolly, and we could go and have lunch together somewhere, and talk about old times. But our lives have drifted apart since those old days. It is partly the fault of the train-service, no doubt. Glad as I should be to see you, I don't like to ask you to come all the way to Petersham to dinner, and if you asked me to Potters Bar—well, I should come, but it would be something of a struggle, and I thank you for not asking me. Besides, we have made different friends now, and our tastes are different. After we had talked about the old days, I doubt if we should have much to say to each other. Each of us would think the other a bit of a bore, and our wives would wonder why we had ever been friends at Liverpool. But don't think I have forgotten you. I just send this card to let you know that I am still alive, still at the same address, and that I still remember you. No need, if we ever do meet, or if we ever want each other's help, to begin by saying: 'I suppose you have quite forgotten those old days at Liverpool.' We have neither of us forgotten; and so let us send to each other, once a year, a sign that we have not forgotten, and that once upon a time we were friends. 'A merry Christmas to you.'"

That is what a Christmas card should say. It is absurd to say this to a man or woman whom one is perpetually ringing up on the telephone; to somebody whom one met last week or with whom one is dining the week after; to a man whom one may run across at the club on almost any day, or a woman whom one knows to shop daily at the same stores as oneself. It is absurd to say it to a correspondent to whom one often writes. Let us reserve our cards for the old friends who have dropped out of our lives, and let them reserve their cards for us.

But, of course, we must have kept their addresses; otherwise we have to print our cards publicly—as I am doing now. "Old friends will please accept this, the only intimation."

The Future

The recent decision that, if a fortune-teller honestly believes what she is saying, she is not defrauding her client, may be good law, but it does not sound like good sense. To a layman like myself it would seem more sensible to say that, if the client honestly believes what the fortune-teller is saying, then the client is not being defrauded.

For instance, a fortune-teller may inform you, having pocketed your two guineas, that a rich uncle in Australia is going to leave you a million pounds next year. She doesn't promise you the million pounds herself; obviously that is coming to you anyhow, fortune-teller or no fortune-teller. There is no suggestion on her part that she is arranging your future for you. All that she promises to do for two guineas is to give you a little advance information. She tells you that you are coming into a million pounds next year, and if you believe it, I should say that it was well worth the money. You have a year's happiness (if that sort of thing makes you happy), a year in which to tell yourself in every trouble, "Never mind, there's a good time coming"; a year in which to make glorious plans for the future, to build castles in the air, or (if your taste is not for castles) country cottages and Mayfair flats. And all this for two guineas; it is amazingly cheap.

And now consider what happens when the year is over. The fortune-teller has done her part; she has given you a year's happiness for two guineas. It is now your uncle's turn to step forward. He is going to give you twenty years' happiness by leaving you a million pounds. Probably he doesn't; he hasn't got a million pounds to leave; he has, in fact, just written to you to ask you to lend him a fiver. Well, surely it is the uncle who has let you down, not the fortune-teller. Curse him by all means, cut him out of your will, but don't blame the fortune-teller, who fulfilled her part of the contract. The only reason why you went to her was to get your happiness in advance. Well, you got it in advance; and seeing

103

that it was the only happiness you got, her claim on your gratitude shines out the more clearly. You might decently send her another guinea.

This is the case if you honestly believe your fortune-teller. Now let us suppose that you don't believe. It seems to me that in this case you are entitled to the return of your money.

Of course, I am not supposing that you are a complete sceptic about these things. It is plainly impossible for a fortune-teller to defraud a sceptic, otherwise than by telling him the truth. For if a sceptic went to consult the crystal, and was told that he would marry again before the month was out, when in fact he was a bachelor, then he has not been defrauded, for he is now in a position to tell all his friends that fortune-telling is absolute nonsense—on evidence for which he deliberately paid two guineas. Indeed, it is just on this ground that police prosecutions seem to me to fail. For a policeman (suitably disguised) pays his money simply for the purpose of getting evidence against the crystal-gazer. Having got his evidence, it is ridiculous of him to pretend that he has been cheated. But if he wasted two guineas of the public money, and was told nothing but the truth about himself and his family, then he could indeed complain that the money had been taken from him under false pretences.

However, to get back to your own case. You, we assume, are not a sceptic. You believe that certain inspired people can tell your future, and that the fee which they ask for doing this is a reasonable one. But on this particular occasion the spirits are not working properly, and all that emerges is that your uncle in Australia— —

But with the best will in the world you cannot believe this. The spirits must have got mixed; they are slightly under-proof this morning; you have no uncle. The fortune-teller gives you her word of honour that she firmly believes you to have at least three uncles in Australia, one of whom will shortly leave you a mill— — It is no good. You cannot believe it. And it seems to me that on the morning's transaction you have certainly been defrauded. You must insist on "a tall dark man from India" at the next sitting.

It is "the tall dark man" which the amateur crystal-gazer really wants. He doesn't want the future. There is so little to foretell in most of our lives. Nobody is going to pay two guineas to be told that he will be off his drive next Saturday and have a stomach-ache on the following Monday. He wants something a little more romantic than that. Even if he is never going to be influenced by a tall dark man from India, it makes life a little more interesting to be told that he is going to be.

For the average man finds life very uninteresting as it is. And I think that the reason why he finds it uninteresting is that he is always waiting for something to happen to him instead of setting to work to make things happen. For one person who dreams of earning fifty thousand pounds, a hundred people dream of being left fifty thousand pounds. I imagine that if a young man went to a crystal-gazer and was told that he would work desperately hard for the next twenty years, and would by that time have earned (and saved) a fortune, he would be very disappointed. Probably he would ask for his money back.

The Largest Circulation

There died recently a gentleman named Nat Gould, twenty million copies of whose books had been sold. They were hardly ever reviewed in the literary papers; advertisements of them rarely appeared; no puffs nor photographs of the author were thrust upon one, Unostentatiously he wrote them—five in a year—and his million public was assured to him. It is perhaps too late now to begin to read them, but we cannot help wondering whence came his enormous popularity.

Mr. Gould, as all the world knows, wrote racing novels. They were called, Won by a Neck, or Lost by a Head, or Odds On, or The Stable-lad's Dilemma. Every third man in the Army carried one about with him. I was unlucky in this matter, for all my men belonged to the other two-thirds; they read detective stories about a certain Sexton Blake, who kept bursting into rooms and finding finger-marks. In your innocence you may think that Sherlock Holmes is the supreme British detective, but he is a child to Blake. If I learnt nothing else in the Army, I learnt that. Possibly these detective stories were a side-line of Mr. Gould's, or possibly my regiment was the one anti-Gould regiment in the Army. At any rate, I was demobilized without any acquaintance with the Won by a Neck stories.

There must be something about the followers of racing which makes them different from the followers of any other sport. I suppose that I am at least as keen on the Lunch Scores as any other man can be on the Two-thirty Winner; yet I have no desire whatever to read a succession of stories entitled How's That, Umpire? or Run Out, or Lost by a Wicket. I can waste my time and money with as much pleasure on the golf-course as Mr. Gould's readers can on the race-course, but those great works, Stymied and The Foozle on the Fifth Tee, leave me cold. My lack of interest in racing explains my lack of interest in racing novels, but why is there no twenty million public for Off-side and Fouled on the Touchline? It is a mystery.

Though I have never read a racing novel, I can imagine it quite easily. Lord Newmarket's old home is mortgaged, mortgaged everywhere. His house is mortgaged, his park is mortgaged, his stud is mortgaged, his tie-pin is mortgaged; yet he wants to marry Lady Angela. How can he restore his old home to its earlier glories? There is only one chance. He must put his shirt (the only thing that isn't mortgaged) on Fido for the Portland Vase. Fido is a rank outsider—most of the bookmakers thought that he was a fox-terrier, not a horse—and he is starting at a thousand to one. When the starting-gate goes up, Fido will carry not only Lord Newmarket's shirt, but Lady Angela's happiness. Was there ever such a race before in the history of racing? Only in the five thousand other racing novels. But Lord Newmarket is reckoning without Rupert Blacknose. Blacknose has not only sworn to wed Lady Angela, but it is he who holds the mortgages on Lord Newmarket's old home. It is at Newmarket Villa that he means to settle down when he is married. If Fido wins, his dreams are shattered. At dead of night he climbs into Fido's stable, and paints him white with a few black splotches. Surely now he will be disqualified as a fox-terrier! He climbs out again, laughing sardonically to himself.... The day of the great race dawns. The Portland Vase! Who has not heard of it? In the far-away Malay Archipelago... in the remotest parts of the Australian bush... in West Kensington... etc., etc. Anyway, the downs were black with people, and the stands were black with more people, and the paddock was packed with black people. But of all these people none concealed beneath a mask of impassivity a heart more anxious than Lord Newmarket's. He wandered restlessly into the weighing-room. He weighed himself. He had gone down a pound. He wandered out again. The downs were still black with humanity. Then came a hoarse cry from twenty thousand throats. "They're off!"

Yes, well, Mr. Gould's novels are probably better than that. But it is a terrifying thought that he wrote a hundred and thirty of them. A hundred and thirty times he described that hoarse cry from twenty thousand throats, "They're off!" A hundred and thirty times he described the downs black with humanity, and the grandstand, and the race itself, and what the bookmakers were saying, and the scene in the paddock. How did he do it? Had he a special rubber stamp for all these usual features, which saved him the trouble of writing them every time? Or did he come quite fresh to it with each book? He wrote five of them every year; did he forget in March what he said in January, only to forget in June and visualize the scene afresh? To describe a race-course a hundred thirty times — what a man!

Yet perhaps, after all, it is not difficult to understand why he was so popular, why he had a following even greater than Mr. Garvice. Mr. Garvice wrote love-stories, stories of that sweet and fair young English girl and that charming, handsome, athletic young Englishman. Every one who is not yet in love, or who is unhappily married, dreams of meeting one or the other, and to read such stories transports the loveless for a moment into the land where they would be. But then there are many more moneyless people in the world than loveless; many more people who want money than who want love. It is these people who are transported by Mr. Nat Gould. He does not (I imagine) write of the stern-chinned, silent millionaire who has forced his way to the top by solid grit; we have no hopes of getting rich that way. But he does (I imagine) write of the lucky fellow who puts his shirt both ways on an outsider and pulls off a cool thousand. Well, that might happen to any of us. It never has yet... but five times a year Mr. Gould carried us away from the world where it never has into that beautiful dream-world where it happens quite naturally. No wonder that he was popular.

The Watson Touch

There used to be a song which affirmed (how truly, I do not know) that every nice girl loved a sailor. I am prepared to state, though I do not propose to make a song about it, that every nice man loves a detective story. This week I have been reading the last adventures of Sherlock Holmes—I mean really the last adventures, ending with his triumph over the German spy in 1914. Having saved the Empire, Holmes returned to his farm on the Sussex downs, and there, for all I mind, he may stay. I have no great affection for the twentieth-century Holmes. But I will give the warmest welcome to as many adventures of the Baker Street Holmes as Watson likes to reconstruct for us. There is no reason why the supply of these should ever give out. "It was, I remember, at the close of a winter's day in 1894"—when Watson begins like this, then I am prepared to listen. Fortunately, all the stories in this last book, with the exception of the very indifferent spy story, are of the Baker Street days, the days when Watson said, "Holmes, this is marvellous!" Reading them now—with, I suppose, a more critical mind than I exhibited twenty years ago—I see that Holmes was not only a great detective, but a very lucky one. There is an occasion when he suddenly asks the doctor why he had a Turkish bath. Utterly unnerved, Watson asks how he knew, to which the great detective says that it is as obvious as is the fact that the doctor had shared a hansom with a friend that morning. But when Holmes explains further, we see how lucky he is. Watson, he says, has some mud on his left trouser; therefore he sat on the left side of a hansom; therefore he shared it with a friend, for otherwise he would have sat in the middle. Watson's boots, he continues, had obviously been tied by a stranger; therefore he has had them off in a Turkish bath or a boot shop, and since the newness of the boots makes it unlikely that he has been buying another pair, therefore he must have been to a Turkish bath. "Holmes," says Watson, "this is marvellous!"

Marvellously lucky, anyway. For, however new his boots, poor old

Watson might have been buying a pair of pumps, or bedroom slippers, or tennis shoes that morning, or even, if the practice allowed such extravagance, a second pair of boots. And there was, of course, no reason whatever why he should not have sat at the side of his hansom, even if alone. It is much more comfortable, and is, in fact, what one always did in the hansom days, and still does in a taxi. So if Holmes was right on this occasion, he was right by luck and not by deduction.

But that must be the best of writing a detective story, that you can always make the lucky shots come off. In no other form of fiction, I imagine, does the author feel so certainly that he is the captain of the ship. If he wants it so, he has it so. Is the solution going to be too easy! Then he puts in an unexpected footprint in the geranium bed, or a strange face at the window, and makes it more difficult, Is the reader being kept too much in the dark? Then a conversation overheard in the library will make it easier for him. The author's only trouble is that he can never be certain whether his plot is too obscure or too obvious. He knows himself that the governess is guilty, and, in consequence, she can hardly raise her eyebrows without seeming to him to give the whole thing away.

There was a time when I began to write a detective story for myself. My murder, I thought, was rather cleverly carried out. The villain sent a letter to his victim, enclosing a stamped addressed envelope for an answer. The gum of the envelope was poisoned. I did not know, nor did I bother to find out, whether it was possible, but this, as I said just now, is the beauty of writing a detective story. If there is no such quick-working poison, then you invent one. If up to the moment when the doubt occurs to you, your villain had been living in Brixton, you immediately send him to Central Africa, where he extracts a poison from a "deadly root" according to the prescription of the chief medicine-man. ("It is the poison into which the Swabiji dip their arrows," you tell the reader casually, as if he really ought to have known it for himself.) Well, then, I invented my poison, and my villain put it on the gum of a self-addressed envelope, and enclosed it with a letter asking for his victim's autograph. He then posted the letter, whereupon a very tragic thing happened.

What happened was that, having left the letter in the post for some years while I formed fours and saluted, I picked up a magazine in the Mess one day and began to read a detective story. It was a very baffling one, and I really didn't see how the murderer could possibly have committed his foul deed. But the detective was on to it at once. He searched the wastepaper basket, and, picking an envelope therefrom, said "Ha!" It was just about then that I said "Ha!" too, and also other things, for my half-finished story was now useless. Somebody else had thought of the same idea. But though I was very sorry for this, I could not help feeling proud that my idea made such a good story. Indeed, since then I have fancied myself rather as a detective-story-writer, and if only I could think of something which nobody else would think of while I was thinking of it, I would try again.

Some Old Companions

In the days of the last-war-but-thirty-seven, when (as you will remember) the Peers were fighting the People, Lord Curzon defended the hereditary system by telling us that it worked very well in India, where a tailor's son invariably became a tailor. The obvious answer, if anyone bothered to give it, was that the tailor's son, having had his career mapped out for him at birth, presumably prepared to be a tailor, whereas a peer's eldest son, as far as one observed, did not prepare to be a statesman. Indeed, the only profession in this country to which one is apprenticed in one's childhood is that of royalty. The future King can begin to learn the "tactful smile," the "memory for faces," the knowledge of foreign languages and orders, almost as soon as he begins to learn anything. He alone need not regret his youth and say, "If only I had been taught this, that, and the other instead!"

These gloomy reflections have been forced on me by the re-discovery of all those educational books which I absorbed, or was supposed to have absorbed, at school and college. They made an imposing collection when I had got them all together; fifty mathematical works by eminent Den, from a well-thumbed, dog's-eared Euclid to a clean uncut copy of Functions of a Quaternion. It is doubtful if you even know what a quaternion is, still less how it functions; probably you think of it as a small four-legged animal with a hard shell. You may be right—it is so long since I bought the book. But once I knew all about quaternions; kept them, possibly, at the bottom of the garden; and now I ask myself in Latin (for I learnt Latin too), "Cui bono?" How much better if I had learnt this, that, and the other instead!

History for instance. How useful a knowledge of history would be to me now. To lighten an article like this with a reference to what Garibaldi said to Cavour in '53; to round off a sentence with the casual remark, "As was the custom in Alexander's day"; to trace back a religious tendency, or a fair complexion, or the price of boots to some barbarian invasion of a thousand years ago—how delightfully easy it would be, I tell myself, to write with such knowledge at one's disposal. One would never be at a loss for a subject, and plots for stories, plays, and historical novels would be piled up in one's brain for the choosing. But what can one do with mathematics—save count the words of an article (when written) with rather more quickness and accuracy than one's fellow writer? Did I spend ten years at mathematics for this? The waste of it!

But perhaps those years were not so wasted as they seem to have been. Not only Functions of a Quaternion, but other of these books, chatty books about hydro-mechanics and dynamics of a particle (no, not an article—that might have been helpful—a particle), gossipy books about optics and differential equations, many of these have a comforting air of cleanness; as if, having bought them at the instigation of my instructor, I had felt that this was enough, and that their mere presence in my bookcase was a sufficient talisman; a talisman the more effective because my instructor had marked some of the chapters "R"—meaning, no doubt, "Read carefully"—and other chapters "RR" or "Read twice as carefully." For these seem to be the only marks in some of the books, and there are no traces of midnight oil nor of that earnest thumb which one might expect from the perspiring seeker after knowledge.

So I feel—indeed, I seem to remember—that the years were not so wasted after all. When I should have been looking after my quaternions, I was doing something else, something not so useful to one who would be a mathematician, but perhaps more useful to a writer who had already learnt enough to count the words in an article and to estimate the number of guineas due to him. But whether this be so or not, at least I have another reason for gratitude that I treated some of these volumes so reverently. For I have now sold them all to a secondhand bookseller, and he at least was influenced by the clean look of those which I had placed upon the top.

So they stand now, my books, in a shelf outside the shop waiting for a new master. Fifteen shillings I paid for some of them, and you or anybody else can get them for three and sixpence, with my autograph inside and the "R" and "RR" of some of our most learned mathematicians. I should like to hear from the purchaser, and to know that he is giving my books as kind a home as I gave them, treating them as reverently, exercising them as gently. He can never be a mathematician, or anything else, unless he has them on his shelves, but let him not force his attentions upon them. Left to themselves they will exert their own influence.

I shall wonder sometimes what he is going to be, this young fellow who is now reading the books on which I was brought up. Spurred on by the differential equations, will he decide to be a lawyer, or will the dynamics of a particle help him to realize his ambition of painting? Well, whatever he becomes, I wish him luck. And when he sells the books again, may he get a better price than I did.

A Haunted House

We have been trying to hide it from each other, but the truth must now come out. Our house is haunted.

Well, of course, anybody's house might be haunted. Anybody might have a headless ghost walking about the battlements or the bath-room at midnight, and if it were no more than that, I should not trouble you with the details. But our house is haunted in a peculiar way. No house that I have heard of has ever been affected in quite this way before.

I must begin by explaining that it is a new house, built just before the war. (Before the war, not after; this is a true story.) Its first and only tenant was a Mrs. Watson-Watson, who lived here with her daughter. Add her three servants, and you have filled the house. No doubt she could have stowed people away in the cellar, but I have never heard that she did; she preferred to keep it for such coal and wood as came her way. When Mrs. Watson-Watson decided six months ago to retire to the country, we took the house, and have lived here since. And very comfortably, except for this haunting business.

As was to be expected, we were busy for the first few weeks in sending on Mrs. Watson-Watson's letters. Gradually, as the news of her removal got round to her less intimate friends, the flow of them grew less, and at last—to our great relief, for we were always mislaying her address—it ceased altogether. It was not until then that we felt ourselves to be really in possession of our house.

We were not in possession for long. A month later a letter arrived for Lady Elizabeth Mullins. Supposing this to be a nom-de-guerre of Mrs. Watson-Watson's, we searched for, and with great difficulty found, the missing address, and sent the letter on. Next day there were two more letters for Lady Elizabeth; by the end of the week there were half a dozen; and for the rest of that month they came trickling in at the rate of one a day. Mrs. Watson-Watson's address was now definitely lost, so we tied Lady-Elizabeth's letters up in a packet and sent them to the ground-landlord's solicitors. Solicitors like letters.

It was annoying at this time, when one was expecting, perhaps, a very important cheque or communication from the Prime Minister, to go downstairs eagerly at the postman's knock and find a couple of letters for Lady Elizabeth and a belated copy of the Church Times for Mrs. Watson-Watson. It was still more annoying, that, just when we were getting rid of Lady Elizabeth, Mr. J. Garcia should have arrived to take her place.

Mr. Garcia seems to be a Spaniard. At any rate, most of his letters came from Spain. This makes it difficult to know what to do with them. There was something clever in Spanish on the back of the last one, which may be the address to which we ought to return it, but on the other hand, may be just the Spanish for "Always faithful" or "Perseverance" or "Down with the bourgeoisie." He seems to be a busier person than Lady Elizabeth. Ten people wrote to him the other week, whereas there were never more than seven letters in a week for her ladyship.

Until lately, I have always been annoyed by the fact that there is no Sunday post in London. To come down to breakfast knowing that on this morning anyhow there is no chance of an O.B.E. takes the edge off one's appetite. But lately, I have been glad of the weekly respite. For one day in seven I can do without the excitement of wondering whether there will be three letters for Mr. Garcia this morning, or two for Lady Elizabeth, or three for Lady Elizabeth, or one for Mrs. Watson-Watson. I will gladly let my own correspondence go in order to be saved from theirs. But on Sunday last, about tea-time, there came a knock at the front-door and the unmistakable scuttle of a letter being pushed through the slit and dropping into the hall, My senses are now so acute in this matter, that I can almost distinguish the scuffle of a genuine Garcia from that of a Mullins or even a Watson-Watson. There was a novelty about this arrival which was interesting. I went into the hall, and saw a letter on the floor, unstamped and evidently delivered by hand. It was inscribed to Sir John Poling.

Will somebody offer an explanation? I have given you our story— leaving out as accidental, and not of sufficient historic interest, the postcard to the Countess of Westbury and the obvious income-tax form to Colonel Todgers, C.B.—and I feel that it is up to you or the Psychical Research Society or somebody to tell us what it all means. My own explanation is this. I think that our house is haunted by ghosts, but by the ghosts of living persons only, and that these ghosts are visible to outsiders, but invisible to the inmates Thus Mr. Lopez, while passing down our street, suddenly sees J. Garcia looking at him from our drawing-room window. "Caramba!" he says, "I thought he was in Barcelona." He makes a note of the address, and when he gets back to Spain writes long letters to Garcia begging him to come back to his Barcelonian wife and family. At another time somebody else sees Sir John Poling letting himself in at the front door with a latch-key. "So that's where he lives now," she says to herself, and spreads the news among their mutual friends. Of course, this is very annoying for us, and one cannot help wishing that these ghosts would confine themselves to one of the back bedrooms. Failing this, they might leave some kind of address in indelible letters on the bath-mat.

Another explanation is that our address has become in some way a sort of typical address, just as "Thomas Atkins" became the typical soldier for the purpose of filling up forms, and "John Doe" the typical litigant. When a busy woman puts our address on an envelope beneath the name of Lady Elizabeth Mullins, all she means is that Lady Elizabeth lives somewhere, and that the secretary had better look up the proper address and write it in before posting the letter. Every now and then the secretary forgets to do this, and the letter comes here. This may be a compliment to the desirability of our house, but it is a compliment of which we are getting tired. I must ask that it should now cease.

Round the World and Back

A friend of mine is just going off for his holiday. He is having a longer holiday than usual this time. Instead of his customary three weeks, he is having a year, and he is going to see the world. He begins with India. Probably some of our Territorials will wonder why he wants to see India particularly. They would gladly give him all of it. However, he is determined to go, and I cannot do less than wish him luck and a safe return.

There are several places to which I should be glad to accompany him, but India is not one of them. Kipling ruined India for me, as I suspect he did for many other of his readers. I picture India as full of intriguing, snobbish Anglo-Indians, who are always damning the Home Government for ruining the country. It is an odd thing that, although I have lived between thirty and forty years in England, nobody believes that I know how to govern England, and yet the stupidest Anglo-Indian, who claims to know all about the proper government of India because he has lived there ten or twenty years, is believed by quite a number of people to be speaking with authority. No doubt my friend will have the decisive word in future in all his arguments on Indian questions with less travelled acquaintances. But he shall not get round me.

From India he goes to China, and thither I would follow him with greater willingness, albeit more tremulously. I can never get it out of my head that the Chinese habitually torture the inquiring visitor. Probably I read the wrong sort of books when I was young. One of them, I remember, had illustrations. No doubt they were illustrations of mediaeval implements; no doubt I am as foolish as the Chinaman would be who had read about the Tower of London and feared to disembark at Folkstone; but it is hard to dispel these early impressions. "Yes, yes," I should say rather hastily, as they pointed out the Great Wall to me, and I should lead the way unostentatiously but quite definitely towards Japan.

Before deciding how long to stay in Japan, one would have to ask oneself what one wants from a strange country. I think that the answer in my case is "Scenery." The customs of Japan, or Thibet, or Utah are interesting, no doubt, but one can be equally interested in a description of them. The people of these countries are interesting, but then I have by no means exhausted my interest in the people of England, and five minutes or five months among an entirely new set of people is not going to help me very much. But a five-second view of (say) the Victoria Falls is worth acres of canvas or film on the subject, and as many gallons of ink as you please. So I shall go to Japan for what I can see, and (since it is so well worth seeing) remain there as long as I can.

I am not sure where we go next. New Zealand, if the holiday were mine; for I have always believed New Zealand to be the most beautiful country in the world. Also it is from all accounts a nice clean country. If I were to arrange a world-tour for myself, instead of following some other traveller about in imagination, my course would be settled, not, in the first place, by questions of climate or scenery or the larger inhabitants, but by consideration of those smaller natives — the Tarantula, the Scorpion, and the Centipede. If I were told that in such-and-such a country one often found a lion in one's bath, I might be prepared to risk it. I should feel that there was always a chance that the lion might not object to me. But if I heard that one might find a tarantula in one's hotel, then that country would be barred to me for ever. For I should be dead long before the beast had got to close quarters; dead of disgust.

This is why South America, which always looks so delightful on the map, will never see me. I have had to give up most of Africa, India (though, as I have said, this is a country which I can spare), the West Indies, and many other places whose names I have forgotten. In a world limited to inhabitants with not more than four legs I could travel with much greater freedom. At present the two great difficulties in my way are this insect trouble, and (much less serious, but still more important) the language trouble. You can understand, then, how it is that, since also it is a beautiful country, I look so kindly on New Zealand.

But I doubt if I could be happy even in a dozen New Zealands, each one more beautiful than the last, seeing that it would mean being away from London for a year. The number of things which might happen in the year while one was away! The new plays produced, the literary and political reputations made and lost, a complete cricket championship fought out; in one's over-anxious mind there would never be such a year as the year which one was missing. My friend may retain his calm as he hears of our distant doings in Kiplingized India, but it would never do for me. Even to-day, after a fortnight in the country, I am beginning to get restless. Really, I think I ought to get back to-morrow.

The State of the Theatre

We are told that the theatre is in a bad way, that the English Drama is dead, but I suspect that every generation in its turn has been told the same thing. I have been reading some old numbers of the Theatrical Magazine of a hundred years ago. These were the palmy days of the stage, when blank verse flourished, and every serious play had to begin like this:

Scene. A place without. Rinaldo discovered dying. Enter Marco.
Mar. What ho, Rinaldo! Lo, the hornéd moon
Dims the cold radiance of the westering stars,
Pale sentinels of the approaching dawn. How now, Rinaldo?
Rin. Marco, I am dying, Struck down by Tomasino's treacherous hand.
Mar. What, Tomasino?
Rin. Tomasino. Ere
The flaming chariot of Phoebus mounts
The vaults of Heaven, Rinaldo will be dead.
Mar. Oh, horror piled on horror! Lo, the moon — —

And so on. The result was called — and I think rightly — "a tragedy." The alternative to these tragedies was a farce, in which everybody went to an inn and was mistaken for somebody else (causing great fun and amusement), the heat and burden of the evening resting upon a humorous man-servant called Trickett (or something good like that). And whether the superior people of the day said that English Drama was dead, I do not know; but they may be excused for having thought that, if it wasn't dead, it ought to have been.

Fortunately we are doing better than that to-day. But we are not doing as well as we should be, and the reason generally given is that we have not enough theatres. No doubt we have many more theatres than we had a hundred years ago, even if you only count those which confine themselves to plays without music, but the

121

mass-effect of all these music-hall-theatres is to make many people think and say that English Drama is (once more) dead.

It is customary to blame the manager for this—the new type of manager, the Mr. Albert de Lauributt who has been evolved by the war. He existed before the war, of course, but he limited his activities to the music-hall. Now he spreads himself over half a dozen theatres, and produces a revue or a musical comedy at each. He does not care for Art, but only for Money. He would be just as proud of a successful production of Kiss Me, Katie, as of Hamlet; and, to do him justice, as proud of a successful production of Hamlet, as of Kiss Me, Katie. But by "successful" he means "financially successful"; no more and no less. He is frankly out for the stuff, and he thinks that it is musical comedy which brings in the stuff.

It seems absurd to single him out for blame, when there are so many thousands of other people in the world who are out for the stuff. Why should Mr. Albert de Lauributt lose two thousand pounds over your or my serious play, when he can make ten thousand over Hug me, Harriet? We do not blame other rich men for being as little quixotic with their money. We do not expect a financier to back a young inventor because he is a genius, in preference to backing some other inventor because he has discovered a saleable, though quite inartistic, breakfast food. So if Mr. de Lauributt produces six versions in his six different theatres of Cuddle Me, Constance, it is only because this happens to be his way of making money. He may even be spending his own evenings secretly at the "Old Vic." For he runs his theatre, not as an artist, but as a business man; and, as any business man will tell you, "Business is business, my boy."

We cannot blame him then. But we can regret that he is allowed to own six different theatres. In Paris it is "one man, one theatre," and if it were so in London then there would be less the matter with the English Drama. But, failing such an enactment, all that remains is to persuade the public that what it really wants is something a little better than Kiss Me, Katie. For Mr. de Lauributt is quite ready to provide Shakespeare, Ibsen, Galsworthy, modern drama, modern comedy, anything you like as long as it brings him in pots of money. And he would probably do the thing well. He would have the sense to know that the producer of Hug Me, Harriet, would not be the best possible producer of The Wild Duck; he would try to get the best possible producer and the best possible designer and the best possible cast, knowing that all these would help to bring in the best possible box-office receipts. Yes, he would do the thing well, if only the public really asked for it.

How can the public ask for it? Obviously it can only do this by staying away from Cuddle Me, Constance, and visiting instead those plays whose authors take themselves seriously, whenever such plays are available. It should be the business, therefore, of the critics (the people who are really concerned to improve the public taste in plays) to lead the public in the right direction; away, that is, from the Bareback Theatre, and towards those theatres whose managers have other than financial standards. But it is unfortunately the fact that they don't do this. Without meaning it, they lead the public the wrong way. They mislead them simply because they have two standards of criticism—which the public does not understand. They go to the Bareback Theatre for the first night of Kiss Me, Katie, and they write something like this:—

"Immense enthusiasm.... A feast of colour to delight the eye. Mr. Albert de Lauributt has surpassed himself.... Delightfully catchy music.... The audience laughed continuously.... Mr. Ponk, the new comedian from America, was a triumphant success.... Ravishing Miss Rosie Romeo was more ravishing than ever... Immense enthusiasm."

On the next night they go to see Mr. A. W. Galsbarrie's new play, Three Men. They write like this:—

"Our first feeling is one of disappointment. Certainly not Galsbarrie at his best.... The weak point of the play is that the character of Sir

John is not properly developed.... A perceptible dragging in the Third Act.... It is a little difficult to understand why.... We should hardly have expected Galsbarrie to have... The dialogue is perhaps a trifle lacking in... Mr. Macready Jones did his best with the part of Sir John, but as we have said... Mr. Kean-Smith was extremely unsuited to the part of George.... The reception, on the whole, was favourable."

You see the difference? Of course there is bound to be a difference, and Mr. A. W. Galsbarrie would be very much disappointed if there were not. He understands the critic's feeling, which is simply that Kiss Me, Katie, is not worth criticizing, and that Three Men most emphatically is. Rut it is not surprising that the plain man-in-the-street, who has saved up in order to take his girl to one of the two new plays of the week, and is waiting for the reviews to appear before booking his seats, should come to the conclusion that Three Men seems to be a pretty rotten play, and that, tired though they are of musical comedy, Kiss Me, Katie, is evidently something rather extra special which they ought not to miss.

Which means pots more money for Mr. Albert de Lauributt.

The Fires of Autumn

The most important article of furniture in any room is the fireplace. For half the year we sit round it, warming ourselves at its heat; for the other half of the year we continue to sit round it, moved thereto by habit and the position of the chairs. Yet how many people choose their house by reason of its fireplaces, or, having chosen it for some other reason, spend their money on a new grate rather than on a new sofa or a grand piano? Not many.

For one who has so chosen his house the lighting of the first fire is something of a ceremony. But in any case the first fire of the autumn is a notable event. Much as I regret the passing of summer, I cannot help rejoicing in the first autumn days, days so cheerful and so very much alive. By November the freshness has left them; one's thoughts go backwards regretfully to August or forwards hopefully to April; but while October lasts, one can still live in the present. It is in October that one tastes again the delights of the fireside, and finds them to be even more attractive than one had remembered.

But though I write "October," let me confess that, Coal Controller or no Coal Controller, it was in September that I lit my first fire this year. Perhaps as the owner of a new and (as I think) very attractive grate I may be excused. There was some doubt as to whether a fireplace so delightful could actually support a fire, a doubt which had to be resolved as soon as possible. The match was struck with all solemnity; the sticks caught up the flame from the dying paper and handed it on to the coal; in a little while the coal had made room for the logs, and the first autumn fire was in being.

Among the benefits which the war has brought to London, and a little less uncertain than some, is the log fire. In the country we have always burnt logs, with the air of one who was thus identifying himself with the old English manner, but in London never—unless it were those ship's logs, which gave off a blue flame and very little else, but seemed to bring the fact that we were an island people more closely home to us. Now wood fires are universal. Whether the air will be purer in consequence and fogs less common, let the scientist decide; but we are all entitled to the opinion that our drawing-rooms are more cheerful for the change.

However, if you have a wood fire, you must have a pair of bellows. I know a man who always calls them "bellus," which is, I believe, the professional pronunciation. He also talks about a "hussif" and a "cold chisel." A cold chisel is apparently the ordinary sort of chisel which you chisel with; what a hot chisel is I never discovered. But whether one calls them "bellows" or "bellus," in these days one cannot do without them. They are as necessary to a wood fire as a poker is to a coal fire, and they serve much the same purpose. There is something very soothing about poking a fire, even if one's companions point out that one is doing it all wrong, and offer an exhibition of the correct method. To play upon a wood fire with a bellows gives one the same satisfaction, and is just as pleasantly annoying to the onlookers. They alone know how to rouse the dying spark and fan it gently to a flame, until the whole log is a triumphant blaze again; you, they tell you, are merely blowing the whole thing out.

It is necessary, then, that the bellows-making industry should revive. My impression is that a pair of bellows is usually catalogued under the heading, "antique furniture," and I doubt if it is possible to buy a pair anywhere but in an old furniture shop. There must be a limit to the number of these available, a limit which has very nearly been reached. Here is a chance for our ironmongers (or carpenters, or upholsterers, or whoever have the secret of it). Let them get to work before we are swamped with German bellows. It is no use to offer us pokers with which to keep our log fires burning; we must have wind. There is one respect in which I must confess that the coal fire has the advantage of the wood fire. If your favourite position is on the hearth-rug with your back to whatever is burning, your right hand gesticulating as you tell your hearers what is wrong with the confounded Government, then it does not greatly matter what brings you that pleasant dorsal warmth which inspires you to such eloquence. But if your favourite position is in an armchair facing the fire, and your customary habit one of passive thought rather than of active speech, then you will not get those visions from the burning wood which the pictures in a coal fire bring you. There are no deep, glowing caverns in the logs from which friendly faces wink back at you as your head begins gently to nod to them. Perhaps it is as well. These are not the days for quiet reflection, but for action. At least, people tell me so, and I am very glad to hand on the information.

Not Guilty

As I descended the stairs to breakfast, the maid was coming up.

"A policeman to see you, sir," she said, in a hushed voice. "I've shown him into the library."

"Thank you," I answered calmly, just as if I had expected him.

And in a sense, I suppose, I had expected him. Not particularly this morning, of course; but I knew that the day was bound to come when I should be arrested and hurried off to prison. Well, it was to be this morning. I could have wished that it had been a little later in the day, when I had more complete command of myself. I wondered if he would let me have my breakfast first before taking me away. It is impossible for an arrested man to do himself justice on an empty stomach, but after breakfast he can play the part as it should be played. He can "preserve a calm exterior" while at the same time "hardly seeming to realize his position"; he can "go quietly" to the police-station and "protest that he has a complete answer to the charge." He can, in fact, do all the things which I decided to do as I walked to the library—if only I was allowed to have my breakfast first.

As I entered the library, I wondered what it was that I had done; or, rather, what it was that I had looked as if I were doing. For that is my trouble—that I look guilty so easily. I never cash a cheque at the bank but I expect to feel a hand on my shoulder and to hear a stern voice saying, "You cummer longer me." If I walk through any of the big stores with a parcel in my hand I expect to hear a voice whispering in my ear, "The manager would like to see you quietly in his office." I have never forged or shoplifted in my life, but the knowledge that a real forger or shoplifter would try to have the outward appearance of a man as innocent as myself helps to give me the outward appearance of a man as guilty as he. When I settle a bill by cheque, my "face-of-a-man-whose-account-is-already-overdrawn" can be read across the whole length of the shop as soon as I enter the door. Indeed, it is so expressive that I had to give up banking at Cox's during the war.

"Good morning," said the policeman. "I thought I'd better tell you that I found your dining-room window open at six o'clock this morning when I came on duty."

"Oh!" I said, rather disappointed.

For by this time I had prepared my speech from the dock, and it seemed a pity to waste it. There is no part quite so popular as that of the Wrongly Accused. Every hero of every melodrama has had to meet that false accusation at some moment during the play; otherwise we should not know that he was the hero. I saw myself in the dock, protesting my innocence to the last; I saw myself entering the witness box and remaining unshaken by the most relentless cross-examination; I saw my friends coming forward to give evidence as to my unimpeachable character....

And yet, after all, what could one's friends say? Imagine yourself in the dock, on whatever charge it may be, and imagine this and that friend coming forward to speak to you. What can they say?

What do they know? They know that you are a bore or not a bore, a grouser or not a grouser, generous or mean, sentimental or cynical, an optimist or a pessimist, and that you have or have not a sense of humour. None of these is a criminal offence. Is there anything else that your friends can say about you which can establish the likelihood of your innocence? Not very much. Nor should we be flattered if there were. When somebody says of us, "Oh, I can read old Jones like a book; I know him inside and out—for the most straightforward, simple creature," we protest indignantly. But if somebody says, "There's a lot more in Jones than you think; I shall never quite understand him," then we look modestly down our nose and tell ourselves that we are Jones, the Human Enigma. Women have learnt all about this. They realize that the best way to flatter us is to say earnestly, with a shake of the head, "Your face is

129

such a mask; I shall never know what you're really thinking." How that makes us purr!

No, our friends cannot help us much, once we are in the dock. They will protest, good friends that they are, that we are utterly incapable of the crime of which we are accused (and in my case, of course, they will be right), but the jury will know that our friends do not really know; or at any rate the jury will guess that we have not asked those of our friends who did know to speak for us. We must rely on ourselves; on our speech from the dock; on our demeanour under cross-examination; on — —

"Your dining-room window open," said the policeman reproachfully.

"I'm sorry," I said; "I won't leave it open again."

Fortunately, however, they can't arrest you for it. So I led the way out of the library and opened the front door. The policeman went quietly.

A Digression

My omnibus left the broad and easy way which leads to Victoria Station and plunged into the strait and narrow paths which land you into the river at Vauxhall if you aren't careful, and I peered over the back to have another look at its number. The road-mending season is in full swing now, but no amount of road-mending could account for such a comprehensive compass as we were fetching. For a moment I thought that the revolution had begun. "'Busful of Bourgeoisie Kidnapped" would make a good head-line for the papers. Or perhaps it was merely a private enterprise. We were to be held for ransom in some deserted warehouse on the margin of the Thames, into which, if the money were not forthcoming, we should be dropped with a weight at the feet on some dark and lonely night.... Fortunately the conductor came up at this stage of the journey and said "Ennimorfairplees," whereupon I laid my fears before him and begged him to let me know the worst. He replied briefly, "Shorerpersher," and went down again. So that was it.

Why is the Shah of Persia so popular? Even in these days when kings are two a penny, and there is a never-ending procession of Napoleons and Nelsons to the Guildhall to receive swords and freedoms and honorary degrees, the arrival of a Shah of Persia stirs the imagination of the man in the street. He feels something of the old thrill. But in the nineties, of course, we talked about nothing else for weeks. "Have you seen the Shah?" was the popular catch-phrase of the day; there were music hall songs about him; he was almost as important as a jubilee.

It is curious that this should have been so, for a Shah of Persia is not really as important as that. There was never a catch-phrase, "Have you seen the French President?" or even "Have you seen the Tsar?" both of whom one would expect to take precedence of a Persian ruler. But they are more commonplace people. The Shah makes his appeal, not on account of his importance but on account of his romantic associations. He fills the mind with thoughts of uncut rubies, diamond-studded swords, Arab chargers, veiled houris, and the very best Persian sherbet. One does not stand outside Victoria in the hope of seeing any of these things in the carriage with him, but one feels that is the sort of man he is, and that if only he could talk English like you or me, he could tell us a story worth the telling. "Hooray for the Shah!"

Seated on my omnibus, and thinking of these things—(we had tacked by this time, and were beating up for Pimlico)—I remembered suddenly a little personal incident in connexion with the visit of that earlier Shah which is not without its moral for all of us. It teaches us the lesson that—well, we can settle this afterwards. Anyway, here is the story.

The Shah of Persia was in England, and all England was talking about him. Naturally, we were talking about him at my private school. I was about nine at the time; it is not the age at which one knows much about high politics, but it is almost the only age when one really knows where Persia is. I have no doubt that we "did" Persia in that term, out of honour to the Shah. One result of all this talk in the school about the Persian Potentate was (as you might expect) that a certain boy was nicknamed "The Shah," presumably on account of some magnificence of person or costume. Now it happened that the school was busying itself just then over some election—to the presidency of the Debating Society, or membership of the Games Committee, or something of that sort—and "The Shah" was a very popular candidate. I was one of his humble but admiring supporters.

Observe me, then, on the polling day, busily at work in a corner of the schoolroom. I am writing in bold capitals on a piece of exercise paper, "Vote for the shah." Having written it, I pinned it proudly up in a corner of the room, and stood back awhile to look at it. My first effort at electioneering. There was no immediate sensation, for everybody else was too busy over his own affairs to notice my little poster, and so I went about from one little knot of talkers to another, hanging shyly on the outskirts in the hope that, when it broke up, I might lead the way casually towards my masterpiece— "VOTE FOR THE SHAH."

Suddenly my attention was attracted to another boy, who, even as I had been a few minutes ago, was now busily writing. I kept my eye on him, and when he had finished his work, and was walking across the room with a piece of paper in his hand, I followed him eagerly. He was at least twelve; I was only nine. Can you wonder that he seemed to me almost the last word in wisdom? So I followed him. Could it really be that my poster had forstalled his? What glory if it were so! He pinned up his notice. He moved away, and I read it. It said: "VOTE FOR THE SHAR."

You can imagine my feelings. I went hot all over. "Shar," of course, not "Shah." How ever could I have been such an idiot as to have thought it was "Shah"? S-h-a-h obviously spelt shash, not shar. How nearly I had exposed my appalling ignorance to my fellows! "Vote for the—"; I blushed again, hardly able to think of it. And oh! how thankful I was now that everybody else had been too busy to read my poster. Hastily I went over to it, and tore it down; hastily I went back to my desk and wrote another poster. Observe me now again. I am writing in bold capitals on a piece of exercise paper: "VOTE FOR THE SHAR."

And the moral? Well, my omnibus has now; fetched its compass round Victoria, we are back on the main route again, and I think I must leave the moral to you.

High Finance

I know very little about the Stock Exchange. I know, of course, that stockbrokers wear very shiny top-hats, which they remove when they sing "God Save the King," as they invariably do in a crisis. When they go out to lunch, the younger ones leave their top-hats behind them, and take the air with plastered polls; and after lunch is over, young and old alike have a round of dominoes before placing threepence under the coffee-cup and returning to business. If business is slack, they tell each other jokes, which get into the papers with some such introduction as, "A good story going the round of the Stock Exchange." Probably it was going the round of the nurseries in 72, but the stockbrokers have been so busy making Consols go up and down that they have not been able to listen to it before. Anyway, the careful man always avoids a good story which is going the round of the Stock Exchange.

But apart from these minor activities of the City, the financial world has always been a mystery to me. To this day I do not understand why Consols go up and down. Perhaps they only go down now, but there was a time when they would be 78 1/4 in the morning, 78 1/2 after the Stock Exchange had returned from its coffee, and 78 when it went out to play dominoes again. When they thudded down to 78, this proved that the Government had lost the confidence of the country. But I never heard an explanation of it all which carried any conviction.

Once I asked a noted financial authority to tell me all about it in words of one syllable. He did his best. He said it was "simply a question of supply and demand." In that case one would expect umbrellas to go up and down according to the weather—I mean, of course, the price of umbrellas. But apparently umbrellas aren't so sensitive as stocks, which are the most sensitive things in the world. In the happy days before the war, when the President of Nicaragua sent a stiff note to the President of Uruguay, Consols immediately dropped a quarter of a point. The President of Uruguay answered, "Sorry, my mistake," and Consols went back again. Evidently, several gentlemen, who would have bought Consols in the ordinary way on that Thursday, decided to buy Haricot Beans instead, as being, I suppose, more useful in the event of a war between Nicaragua and Uruguay. So Consols feeling the neglect, went down. But on the Friday, as soon as Uruguay had apologized, the gentlemen who had just sold the Haricot Beans hurried out to buy Consols, as being quite safe again now that there was no more chance of war. So Consols went cheerfully up again. You see?

But the financial problem is getting very much more difficult than this, The vagaries of Consols, or even of the reputed gold-mine in which I once had shares—(this is a sad story, but, fortunately, when they had dropped to six-and-sixpence, there was a demand for them by a man called Wilkinson, poor fellow, which arrested the fall just long enough for me to get out. They are now three a penny, so I hope Wilkinson found a demand, too)—well, then, even the vagaries of the West African market are a simple matter compared with the vagaries of the Exchange. The mystery of the mark, for instance, is so utterly beyond that, in trying to understand it, I do not even know where to begin. I see no mental foothold anywhere.

The mark, we are told, is now worth tuppence-ha'penny. Why? I mean, who said so? Who is it who arranges these things? Is it Rockefeller or one of the Geddeses or Samuel Gompers—a superman of some kind? Or is it a Committee of the Stock Exchange and Greenwich Observatory? And how does it decide? Does it put a mark up for auction and see what the demand is like? Or does it decide on moral grounds? Does it say contemptuously, "Oh, I should think about tuppence-ha'penny, and serve 'em dashed well right for losing the war"?

Let us go slowly, and see if we can make any sense of it. Suppose that I produce something worth a shilling, something, that is, which I can sell in this country for a shilling—a blank verse tragedy, say. Let us suppose also that, having received the shilling, I propose to buy a bag of nuts. A German offers me a mark for my tragedy. Now that mark has got to be spent in Germany by somebody; not, of course, necessarily by me. I probably hand it to Thomas Cook or his Son, who gives it to somebody else, who eventually takes it back to Germany again. Obviously, then, what I have to consider, when I am offered a mark instead of the customary shilling for my blank verse, is this: "Can this mark purchase a similar-sized bag of nuts in Germany?" If the answer is "Yes," then the mark is worth a shilling; if the answer is that it will only buy a bag of about a fifth of the English size, then the mark is worth tuppence-ha'penny.

Well, is everything in Germany five times as dear as it is in England? No. Not by any means. If a mark is regarded as tuppence-ha'penny, everything is extraordinarily cheap; much cheaper than in England. Also it occurs to me suddenly that if this were the way in which the pundits decided upon the price of the mark and the franc and the peseta and the cowrie-shell, then the price of living in every country would be exactly the same, and we should have nowhere to retire to when the taxes were too high. Which would be absurd. So we must have done the sum wrong. Let us try again.

The price of the mark (this is our new theory) depends on the amount of goods which Germany is exporting. A German offers me a mark for my tragedy, but if no other German has got anything to give me, or Thomas Cook or his Son, in exchange for that mark, then the mark is obviously no good to us. If, then, we say that the mark is worth tuppence-ha'penny, we mean that Germany is importing (or buying) five times as much as she is exporting (or selling). Similarly, when the rouble was about ten a penny, Russia was importing a hundred times as much as she was exporting. But she was not importing anything then because of the blockade. Therefore—no, it's no good. You see, we can't do it. We shall have to stand about on the Brighton road until one of those stockbrokers comes by. He will explain it to us.

But perhaps a better man to consult in these matters of High Finance is the Strong Man whom we see so often upon the stage.

Sometimes he builds bridges, and sometimes he makes steel, but the one I like best is the one who controls the markets of the world. He strides to the telephone and says grimly down it: "Sell Chilled Tomatoes.... No.... Yes... Keep on selling," and in far-away Nan-Kang-Foo a man shoots himself. He had too many Chilled Tomatoes—or too few.

But the Strong Man goes on his way. He is married to a young and beautiful girl, whom he has adored silently for years. He has never told her; partly because he thought it would not be fair to her, partly because he knows it would spoil the play. He is too busy to see much of her, but sometimes they meet at dinner, and then he strokes her head and asks her kindly what she is doing that evening. Probably she is going out with George B. Pusher. What else could you expect? All the time when Staunton is buying Tomatoes and Salmon and Tintacks and Locomotives and Peanuts and lots of things that he doesn't really want, George B. Pusher is in attendance on the Heroine.

There is a terrible scene when Staunton discovers what is going on. Who is this puppy? George B. Pusher? That settles it. He will ruin Pusher.

He sells Tomatoes. Pusher hasn't got any. He buys Raspberry Jam. Pusher doesn't want any. Damn the fellow, he refuses to be ruined. Everybody is shooting himself except Pusher.

At last. Wire Netting! Why didn't he think of Wire Netting before? He buys all the Wire Netting that there is. Then he sells it all. George R. Pusher is ruined. He comes round to beg for mercy.

Now, perhaps, if we listen very carefully, we shall understand how it is all done.

Secret Papers

The cabinet, or whatever I am to call it, has looked stolidly at me from the corner of the library for years. It is nothing more than a row of pigeon-holes in which I keep my secret papers. At least, the man who sold it to me recommended it for this purpose, dwelling lovingly as he did so upon the strength of the lock. So I bought it—in those first days (how far away!) when I came to London to set the Thames on fire.

It was not long before I lost the key. I made one or two half-hearted efforts to get into it with a button-hook; but, finding that the lock lived up to its reputation, I resigned myself to regarding it for the future as an article for ornament, not for use. In this capacity it has followed me about from house to house. As an ornament it is without beauty, and many people have urged me to throw it away. My answer has been that it contained my secret papers. Some day I would get a locksmith to open it, and we should see what we should see.

The war being over, I came into the library and sat down at my desk. Perhaps it was not too late, even now, to set the Thames on fire. I would write an incendiary article on—what? The cabinet caught my eye. I went idly up to it and pulled at the drawers, before I remembered that it was locked. And suddenly I was annoyed with it for being locked; the more I pulled at it, the more I was annoyed; and I ended up by telling it with some heat that, if it persisted in its defiant attitude, I would shoot it down with my revolver. (This is how the hero breaks his way into the room wherein the heroine is immured, and I have often envied him.)

However, the revolver was not necessary. The lock surrendered, after a short struggle, to the poker. For the first time for seventeen years my secret papers were before me. Can you not imagine how eagerly I went through them?

They were a strange collection, these trifles which had (I suppose) seemed so important to me seventeen years ago. There was the inevitable dance programme, covered with initials which must have stirred me delightfully once, but now left me cold. There was a receipt from a Cambridge tailor, my last outstanding Cambridge bill, perhaps—preserved as a sign that I was now free. There was a notice of a short-story competition, stories not to exceed 5000 words; another of a short-sketch competition, sketches not to exceed 1200 words. Apparently I was prepared to write you anything in those days. There was an autograph of a famous man; "Many thanks" and the signature on a postcard, I suppose I had told him that I admired his style, or that I proposed to model myself on him, or had bought his last book, or—who knows? At any rate, he had thanked me.

There were letters from editors; editors whom I know well now, but who in those distant days addressed me as "Sir," and were mine faithfully. They regretted that they could not use the present contribution, but hoped that I would continue to write. I continued to write. Trusting that I would persevere, they were mine very truly. I persevered. Now they are mine ever. From what a long way off those letters have come. "Dear Sir," the Great Man wrote to me, and overawed I locked the precious letter up. Yesterday I smacked him on the back.

There was a list of my first fifteen contributions to the Press. Three of them were accepted; two of the three appeared in a paper which immediately went bankrupt. For the fifteenth I seem to have received fifteen shillings. A shilling an attempt, you see, for those early efforts to set the Thames on fire. Reading the titles of them, I am not surprised. One was called (I blush to record it) "The Diary of a Free-Lance." Was there ever a literary aspirant who did not begin with just such an article on just such a subject?—a subject so engagingly fresh to himself, so hackneyed to the editor. I have returned a hundred of them since without a word of encouragement to the writers, blissfully forgetful of the fact (now brought to light) that I, too, had begun like that.

And last of all, in this locked cabinet I came upon an actual contribution, one of the fifteen which had gone the rounds and had been put away, perhaps for a re-writing.... Dear, dear! I must have been very hopeful in those days. Youth and hope—I am afraid that those were my only qualifications for setting the Thames on fire.

Yet I was very scornful of editors seventeen years ago. The outsider, I held forth, was not given a chance; the young writer with fresh ideas was cold-shouldered. Well, well! Reading this early contribution of mine seventeen years later, reading again what editors had to say about it, I am no longer scornful of them. I can only wonder why they hoped that I would go on writing.

But I shall not throw the broken cabinet away, even though it is no longer available for secret papers. It must continue to sit in a corner of the library, a corrective against secret pride.